WOLF CURSE

MIDNIGHT WOLF CURSE: BOOK 1

T.M. CARUANA

WOLF CURSE

MIDNIGHT WOLF CURSE SERIES
BOOK 1

T. M. CARUANA

First Printing: March 2022
KDP Publishing

ISBN: 9798421370574

CHAPTER 1

It's the moment just before death that I fear the most. The healing energies are the hardest to craft, and weaving the yellow spell cord hurts like a fire burning from within you. But killing someone with a blue spell cord is much worse. Your blood becomes as cold as ice as the cord makes impact with enemy skin.

Fae don't even talk about the red cord.

Right now though, there was a need for a substantial yellow healing cord. The limp rabbit in my hand had been wounded by claws dug deep into its flesh. Four cuts ran down its neck and onto one of its front paws.

I sighed and looked up at my father. "Why would anyone do this without first blessing it in a Fae Temple?"

"It looks as if a big beast was hungry."

That made me worry my biggest fear had come to fruition: that a wolf-shifter had strayed into Fae territory.

Andreas and Vargo; our bodyguards, only shrugged their shoulders as I met their gazes, as if a hurt animal was just a part of the circle of life.

I looked up and deeper into the woods amongst bushy silver birch trees. The wolves could be hiding behind any and every tree, boulder or incline in the ground. The Skyland City wolves were far friendlier than Alpha Skully's crew, but I didn't fancy running into any of them. Whichever Alpha the wolves worked for, they wouldn't attack alone, they were always out in a large pack hunting together. I couldn't see anyone right now, though. Nature was soundless; no wind caught in the leaves and the spring sun was gently warming my back.

I focused back onto my hand where the rabbit lay damaged and pushed down onto the brown furball's stomach with two fingers, hoping the tiny thing would take in air whilst Father worked on weaving yellow magic by rubbing his fingertips together. He worked the cord so fast I could never have been able to keep up with him. As the cord grew longer, he rolled the glowing thread between his palms.

Father lowered himself to sit on his knees next to me, his black hair falling to his chest and his dark eyes as serene as the depths of the ocean.

"Here," he said, handing the yellow lasso to me. "Keep the energy's momentum going. You can do this."

"Me?" I gasped as the magic snake slithered over to my palm, looping down between my fingers.

The cords I was used to were shorter, and the

victims were not usually this close to death.

This is going to hurt.

I breathed deeply, anxiety filling my chest. I wasn't ready for this. I pinned the edge of the cord to the rabbit's shoulder with the thumb of the hand I was holding it in, and with my other hand, I started to wind the cord's length around the body. The whirlwind of emotions causing havoc in my stomach took up speed as I completed the first step.

A shadow was cast over us. My bodyguard Vargo in his iron suit and stony mien towered over Father.

He looked worriedly to-and-fro between my father's face and the glowing magic. "My king, are you sure about this? It's a very long cord for the princess."

"Of course he is, Vargo," answered Andreas, stepping up behind my father. "Athroxane, heir to the Fairola throne, was made for this."

I smiled at his optimism. "Being Father's best friend, I believe you to be somewhat biased, Andreas. And how many times do I have to tell you to call me Roxie when I'm not wearing the court furs? I leave that life behind when I'm off the castle grounds."

"As you wish, my fae princess," he said, his red eyes glistening as he bowed, pushing his black cape aside.

I rolled my eyes at him before focusing back on the rabbit, whose time was on a short countdown. I looked up at my father, and he nodded.

I closed my eyes, cradling the little life in my hands. "Sinsra livris meris."

The unexpected intensity of the fire storming through my blood gave the impression that my veins were bursting. I hesitated, but knew I had to repeat the spell until the wound was healed. The more magic

I added, the more it was going to hurt.

"Sinsra livris meris!" I shouted, as if the strength of my voice could overpower the pain from the energy.

The heat rose up my spine, and in my imagination I could smell the fire that ate away my vertebrae, blackening my bones. The pain only seared deeper and deeper.

Abruptly, the sharp pains vanished, my healing subject torn out of my hands. I looked up and as Andreas finished the spell, the little creature snapped back to life, looking around confusedly before hopping off on its small paws, skipping into the undergrowth that lined the path. Father was staring at his best friend with lowered eyebrows and with clenched teeth as Andreas caught his breath.

"You interfered with a royal order." Father's voice was grim.

This was one thing he couldn't turn a blind eye to, not even for his best friend.

"The cord was too potent. You should have removed it before I did."

"That was my decision to make!"

"She may be your daughter, Trevor, but she is my princess to protect."

"I'm your King! Don't forget that!" Father blared, but quickly calmed somewhat. "You know what this means," Father said through tightly clenched teeth. "A brand line."

"I know," Andreas said, unbothered and pushed up his short sleeve where on his arm there were already four lines running across his biceps. "It's not the first time you have been wrong."

I wanted to plead with Father to forgive him this

once, but I knew the Fae law. It was followed without exceptions. He was going to brand Andreas.

CHAPTER 2

"I'm never wrong," Father muttered as he spun a blue cord to life. It was short and didn't hold a huge amount of poisonous magic, but enough to punish Andreas and mark his skin for life.

Father latched the cord around Andreas's arm with a snap. Andreas moaned softly but held the screams in. Like sizzling cold water on a hot stone, the cord melted through his flesh and integrated with his blood. It left a fifth black scar just below the others. Andreas seemed unperturbed, as he rolled down his sleeve, grinning smugly at his fae king.

His strength really impresses me.

It was expected from his gene pool, though. His ancestors had all served the royal family as the King and Queen's security detail, so he and Father had practically grown up side by side since my father was only a young prince. I had heard worse stories about their pranks when they were boys; leaving permanent scars on each other was not uncommon.

Nothing more was said about it as Father turned around, heading south. The four of us carried on walking along a well-trodden bridleway that led home. We were on our way home from hunting for treasures in Qualmar; the forsaken city across the sea. Father loved to look for old relics and valuable artefacts forged by the blacksmiths and artists from long ago.

Admittedly, I did too.

They seemed to have taken greater pride in their handiwork, and most of them also contained valuable gems that could be traded for a good price on today's market. Although, Father seemed to want to keep all the treasures for himself, just to gawk at when he needed his spirit lifted.

Our quest had been long but fruitful. My father's client had offered a lot of money for him to go and retrieve the relic of a golden crown that had once belonged to an ancient Fae King on the other side of the Fairola Sea. It had been buried in ruins outside Qualmar City, and we had dug for days between rocks, mud and the bones of the dead. My hands were still swollen and sore. Father refused to allow me to use a spade, no matter how blunt it was, as it might damage the artefacts and devalue them. After what had seemed like an eternity, we had finally found the Fae King's corpse, or at least I had assumed the bones were his, as a golden crown was still sitting on top of the fleshless skull. But nothing fazed Andreas, he had simply picked up the skull and prized the crown off, dumping the head back into the mud. We had also found gold coins, a dagger covered with sapphires and a large seer pendant made out of malachite from the region.

Now, we hiked on terrain to the north of my castle, and I knew we were soon going to arrive at the forking path eastwards. Then we only needed to pass Lady Svala's mansion, and I should be able to see the golden flag poles on the top of the blue domed roofs.

It was at Lady Svala's where we stopped for our royal transformation when we hunted for artefacts in the north. She had always been discreet in offering a stable for our horses and a coat hook for our court furs.

She understood the pressure of fame. Her parents had died in an ambush by Master Crowland's men; he was a man who was nothing more than a self-proclaimed warden of the east. I had never seen him, but he was said to be a mercenary dressed in stolen gems. Ting Svala was only thirteen when she became the lady of the mansion and the warden of the district in the north. Lord Givony guarded the midlands all the way to the west until you reached the Fairola Sea, and Lady Chary protected the south.

Lord Givony and Lady Chary also, of course, gave us accommodation when we visited, because no one dared turn away the King, but they were less discreet about our stay. They wanted extravagance and to host feasts and balls, expecting us to stay for at least a few days or they would be offended. Those sorts of things bored my father so he tended to avoid visiting them more than necessary. Father also always seemed to get into disputes with Lord Givony who continuously asked for my hand. Father never told me why he refused the offer and I never asked. I didn't want to marry him anyway as Lord Givony was a man of many faces that I could not read, and none which I liked.

Although Lord Givony was sly, it was nothing compared to the hard façade of Lady Chary; her eyes could really stare daggers at you. Her hair was braided back and hidden under a thin steel helmet that looked like spiky jewellery. The scariest part about her was her fascination with her reptile pets. She always had something slithering around her neck or crawling up her arm. I kid you not, her pupils were formed in slits just like a snake, ogling its prey, looking to pounce upon it at any moment, and swallow it whole. It creeped me out even thinking about it.

Ting Svala was the youngest warden there had been throughout our entire history, and was rarely seen in public. She kept to herself, dressing in black and living in the shadows. Every time I met her, it felt like she was looking at me over her shoulder and from behind her black, sleek hair, already on her way to be somewhere else. She never approached me, or gave me her full attention. Although, it suited me because she didn't blabber about my real identity and how I concealed my true look under the court furs and wig.

At the junction of the forking path, we followed the narrow bridleway that was going to lead us to the back of the mansion close to the stables; a path that carried on and eventually ended by the shore of Svala Lake. As many believed the place to be haunted, the mansion had no gates or protection from intruders, and it seemed too far out of the way to attract the attention of Master Crowland.

From the path, we crossed the lawn towards the stables, that were located in a separate building from the main home itself; a massive rectangular building where I had once counted eighty-nine windows on its front façade alone.

I rushed through the stable doors, longing to see Mazzi again; a mare I had bred myself and who had been with me since she was a foal. Her grey fur and equally grey mane made her look like a ghost-horse risen up from the land of the dead.

I smiled as I saw 'boy Matthews', as he was known; a stable boy, who was actually not a boy anymore, leading Mazzi towards me. Matthews wasn't a man who bowed for anyone, and with that body I completely forgot that he ought to. His overalls had been stripped off halfway down his chest with the sleeves tied low around his rippled abdomen. The biceps on his right arm, hoisted so that he could hold on to Mazzi's throatlatch, bulged like the hills located at the back of the Fairola Castle. The other arm featured an elaborate abstract tattoo.

His muddy knee-high boots clomped over the floor in a different rhythm to Mazzi's hooves, but I was still dumbstruck by the time he was close enough to pierce me with his sapphire blue eyes.

"Princess, you're back, I was just about to take Mazzi out for grazing. Should I prepare her for immediate departure instead?"

Before I got to grips with my ability to speak, Andreas replied over my shoulder.

"Ready the King's horse too. Vargo and I will do our horses ourselves, as we want to get going as soon as possible."

The men were experienced and once they got to work, it wasn't long before all the horses were saddled and bridled, loaded with chunky saddlebags, and supplies or artefacts were laid over their rears. I had arranged my black wig into place and coated my shoulders with layers of fur that both warmed and decorated my stature.

Andreas, used to walking first, gave his stallion a sharp kick in the ribs to get him to move. "Let's go horse!"

Andreas never named his horses, and he had had many. He said they were a mode of transportation, not a friend, and he always kept calling them; the horse, good creature, or filthy thing, and had never understood the bond I had with Mazzi. She was my baby and I dressed her in silks and gold jewels that were more fanciful than anything I bestowed upon my servants.

A gallop didn't seem fast enough, as I was longing terribly for a hot bath, my soft night gown and my bed. When I took on the role as an artefact hunter, I couldn't enjoy such luxuries on my journeys with my father. A little dirt under my nails had never fazed me, but even a beggar had his limits.

When I finally saw the bridge leading to the golden arch frame, where the gates were open, ready for our arrival, my spirits lifted; even more so when the fanfare of trumpets played the royal welcome. I stretched tall in the saddle as Mazzi's hooves clattered over the cobblestones, and the sense of 'home' engulfed me. Guards were bowing at the top of the grey stone battlements, framed by railings made from gold. The blue domed roofs of the towers were only a shade darker than the sky and my fiery pride felt as burning red as the dungeon tower; a tower that rose higher than the others and was painted in red to symbolise the spilling of traitors' blood.

A line of servants awaited our arrival in the

courtyard; the four court members with their serious expressions on their faces, and my handmaiden, 'merry' Kerri, were amongst them. Kerri had dressed in fashionable robes as always, her current garment being in a teal colour with a delicately embroidered wide hem. The top layer of her hair had been swirled into a bun clamped with a golden jewel while the rest of the black hair cascaded down to her waist. Her jaw was square and her eyebrows full, making it hard to determine whether she looked like a feminine man or a masculine woman.

Jayme J was the stable boy who attended to Mazzi; not at all like Matthews, but a boy of twelve summers. His father was the stable master and had trained him well, so I couldn't complain. He was always on time, was clean, dressed handsomely, and his manners were second to none.

He lifted his beret to greet me and took hold of the reins. I dismounted in one fluid movement and instantly had Kerri at my side. Before I knew it, Vargo was also there, closely guarding my back.

I removed my burgundy leather gloves and passed them to Kerri. "I'll need a hot bath with rose scented oils."

"Yes, Your Royal Highness," she chirped and fell into step behind me and Vargo.

"Princess!" Alcar Montegrief, the counsellor who believed himself to be the most important of the court members, called for my attention. "I'm afraid we have some urgent matters that need attending to at the court before you retire."

Alcar had used the most eloquent pronunciations in his words and I just knew I couldn't get away from this one; no matter how hard I wished he would wait until tomorrow.

"Your Majesty," he then greeted my father as he jumped off his horse.

"What's the urgency, Alcar?"

"Your Majesty, I believe that to be a matter for inside the walls of the court and away from prying ears. But I can assure you the matter is most pressing."

"Very well," Father sighed, "Summon the Courtess, the Master of Coins, the Spell Master and the Commander of the Palace Guards to court, and we will convene momentarily."

All the four counsellors stood straight, like stuck up snobs holding their breaths, but it was Alcar who conveyed the message.

"Your Majesty, The Commander of the Guard had to take action in your absence. He has led a battalion to the Wolf Temple."

Father's temper exploded. "Our commander, on wolf territory! What the hell's going on?"

CHAPTER 3

"There was a letter delivered, Your Majesty. The Commander read it…" Alcar glanced around at the other servants, "but we should really discuss this in court."

"Even the dead wouldn't wait for court in the light of this. I must recall the troops or there will be war. Athroxane!"

I snatched my leather gloves out of Kerri's hands, rushing towards Mazzi. "Coming Father." All hope of having a calm evening with a hot bath was shattered.

Andreas's horse neighed as he harshly veered it around, setting off at a gallop after Father. Vargo gave me a leg up on Mazzi and was up on his horse before I had even got mine in motion.

"Ya, ya!" I kicked my heels into Mazzi's flank and sped after Father and Andreas.

I couldn't tell whether it was my heart, or Vargo's

horse's hooves behind me, that pounded in my ears. This wasn't going to be a quest like the others with my father; this was serious. The Commander had trespassed on wolf shifter territory. On treasure hunts, we always stayed within the parameters of safety, this time, we weren't avoiding the danger; we were heading straight into the heart of it.

We soon arrived at the edge of the Fairola jungle, and my aches and pains disappeared in a rush of adrenaline as we spared no time to rest but barged forwards on foot, having left our horses to graze on the other side of the dense vegetation. The humid air trapped inside the thick greenery that was tunnelling around us made it hard to breathe. Every tree, with its twisting limbs, either blocked our way or revealed a new path to tread.

It would be easy to get lost if you didn't know the way. I took high steps to follow my father, ensuring I wouldn't trip over any curling tree roots hidden under the clusters of tropical plants and colourful flowers. The pollen that floated in the air glittered like a thousand shining stars as they were intercepted by the few sun rays, which had managed to penetrate the canopy roof. Butterflies and birds fluttered around us relishing the light – the sight of them was a good indication that we were trekking close to the river as the insects never drifted too far away from it.

Then again, neither did the wild cats, baboons, or the wolves as they battled for the same luscious territory. The other animals, who were lower down in the food chain, strayed farther away from the river and only circled back when they needed fresh water. Just like us Fae did.

A dimness like the murky light during a cloudy

day, had swept over the forest by the time we reached the river in the west. The river fractured the two territories, and we were about to cross that line. When I saw that river, warning bells rang on high alert in my mind.

Never cross that boundary!

Father had forbidden me time and time again, not ever to go anywhere near this boundary. Fae didn't belong on the other side of it – on the other side, we were the game and not the hunters.

I wanted to turn back. I was already exhausted after our recent treasure hunt, and there was only one other area that I despised more: Alpha Mounty's territory in the volcano pass in the south. That place even terrified my inner diva.

But so far, we were still on Fae territory; all but my toes that I dipped in the ice-cold spring water dividing the lands between wolf and Fae. It wasn't as cold as holding a blue magic cord, but I would never dip more than my toes into this temperature. The shallow stream that rippled over my toes and pebbles was as clear as the purest glass, flowing from the Fairola jungle in the north to Alpha Mounty's volcano district in the south.

I cupped my hands to pick up water to drink, seeing a wavering reflection of myself in my palms. I sunk my lips under the surface to suck it all into my mouth. It was so refreshing I almost forgot the imminent hardships ahead. Nonetheless, I was reminded that we weren't on safe ground when Vargo's boots appeared in my peripheral view as I sat squatted down.

"Princess, we should move away from the open," Vargo warned.

"Give me a moment, Vargo," I snapped, tired of him still seeing me as the small child I was when we'd first met. "Are you not going to drink?"

He hunched down beside me without his gaze losing its focus on the jungle on the other side of the river.

"We must be quick, Princess."

"Relax Vargo," Andreas said, squatting down on my other side. "The entire Fae guard is out in these woods on their way to the Wolf Temple. They are probably only a whistle away."

Father grunted at the remark. "Are they faster than the baboons, though?" he challenged as he too drank his fill.

Andreas turned his head pensively. "Then Roxie will be the only survivor, as I've seen her run faster than a Fae on fire when cook Clarence catches her nicking chocolates from the kitchen."

I giggled in my hand. "And she's more vicious than a baboon when she snags me, I'll tell ya!"

Father and Andreas laughed; they knew what I was talking about.

Big, brutish, and totally belligerent, Clarence would be a good match with Vargo; he didn't have any humour either. Some said his heart was as black as his hair.

I didn't even get a smile out of Vargo. He stretched out his hand to me, his face pure with duty. "Princess, let me help you cross the river."

"Why? Not even a baby ant could drown in it. I think I can manage to skip across it without suffering fatal injuries."

I put my boots back on, tying the leather all the way up to my knees. I loved those boots. The bleached horse skin was even whiter than my hair. I stood and flicked my hair so it spread over my shoulders.

"Please," Vargo pleaded, holding out his hand. "The stones can be slippery."

I didn't want to offend his honour, so I took his hand. He squeezed it too hard over mine as we suddenly heard a sharp baboon cry. We all looked up at the treetops. What frightened me more than the actual notion of company was that it sounded like a warning scream rather than a hunting call.

We aren't the ones being hunted; the baboons are.

Whatever was coming after them, making hundreds of balls of brown fur swing past us, wasn't going to be child's play for us four either.

Vargo yanked his bow over his head and anchored an arrow into position. Andreas unsheathed his sword to hold it up in front of him, and Father started to weave a blue cord.

I had just frozen, but the fervour of terror warmed my chest around my thumping heart. My eyes darted from bush to tree to rocks, trying to establish from where the beast might attack.

CHAPTER 4

I managed to get my wits together and slid an arrow from the quiver on my back to anchor in my bow, ready to shoot. My pulse was still racing when the sound of the stressed baboons faded.

What was going to be creeping out of the long grass?

Beige fur and bright yellow eyes swished past within the dense vegetation. It had been so fast I couldn't see where it had gone and I swept my arms along, aiming my arrow at the swaying tall grass. A large cat stepped out into the open, glaring at us. She pumped her paws at the ground, her shoulders bobbing up and down in concentration. By the look of her ribs she appeared starved, but she planned to pounce no matter what the odds were. It was do or die.

These wild cats were fast and strong and could take down one or two Fae easily, but we were four

Fae. She took her time inspecting us, obviously knowing she would need to be cunning to win.

Father's cord was the length of an arm by the time he had to stop to rest his energies.

Vargo turned his head in Father's direction. "Shall I fire, My King?"

"No, wait until she has decided to attack. If you miss, there is a good chance she would be quick enough to harm one of us before we have her under control. Athroxane, you give it a shot; it'll be good practice."

The feline hissed at us like a cat would at its master, who had suggested giving her a bath.

"Me?" I didn't want to kill it, and I didn't like doing the blessing ritual to honour its life afterwards. "And what then? We would have to drag her with us on the entire hike to the Wolf Temple?"

Andreas flashed a grin. "Well, she is lighter than any of us," he joked, but I understood his point.

If I didn't kill it and it killed one of us, we would have to drag a friend to the temple instead, so I tightened the string, supported the knuckle of my thumb on my cheek, and closed one eye. With my open eye, I looked into the wild yellow globes. She could be a mother, a passer-by, or an innocent not even intending to strike and I was prepared to defy the law of life that the holy Fae Mother had created.

I hesitated, tasting bile raise up in my throat to coat my tongue. My muscles had started to give in and my hands had begun shaking. My aim couldn't possibly stay true now, but if I missed, and Vargo missed, she would dig sharp claws into Andreas, who was standing closest to her.

I couldn't hold on to the feather any longer as

quivering muscles compelled my fingers to release the arrow. The white feather whizzed past my eye and the black arrowhead brushed the wild cat's back before drilling itself into the ground.

I'd missed.

The cat jumped at Andreas so quickly that Vargo couldn't release his arrow in the fear of making Andreas the target. Paws with extended claws tore Andreas's clothes and blood stained the fabric. Father launched himself fearlessly over the beast, strapping the blue cord around her neck. He screamed as the magic froze his blood; that's how I was certain it was a strong cord he had woven. The cat roared too, its life draining, sucked up by Fae Magic.

The muscly cat twisted as she writhed in pain. She swept her front paw around her back to rid herself of her enemy, striking the side of Father's torso. He stumbled to the ground and the cat flew at him like a full-fledged eagle before I could load another arrow. Vargo barged towards them with a bull-like charge, circled the feline's waist and wrestled her to the ground, not hesitating to sacrifice his life for the royal family; he never had.

I was still aiming my arrow, but didn't get a clear angle to shoot. Andreas raced towards the fight, bending down to pick up his sword where he had dropped it earlier and jammed the blade into the cat's side before the animal could sink its fangs into Vargo's neck.

The beast slumped on top of Vargo – there was no more sign of life. My knees buckled and, as I dropped onto my bottom, my lungs emptied from the relief.

It was over.

Danger averted.

For now.

Hopefully, the baboons wouldn't return to see what had become of the wild cat, to see it dead and us alive, and no longer be afraid of attacking us.

Andreas helped Vargo up onto his feet. "Thank you, Master Blackstorm," Vargo remarked.

Andreas moaned a reply of welcome and clutched his side, his hand coming out bloody from under his cloak when he brought it out again.

Father glowered at me.

"You missed." He pointed at Andreas's side. "You'll heal that."

Andreas sat down on a knee-high rock. He loved being glorious and tough, but also adored receiving the gentle care of women. Father didn't like it when his attention was directed at me, but this time it was my fault to correct; my wound to heal. I could be sure that Father was going to put me in extra archery lessons when we got back home to the castle.

"Where were your guards, My King?" Andreas mocked, as he lifted his well woven tunic to expose his damaged flesh to me.

"They are probably defending my honour."

I didn't want to look up at the men and just hoped Andreas was not going to challenge Father's comment. I poked extra hard at Andreas's raw flesh to distract him. He moaned, twisting his head down to give me a questioning stare.

I averted my gaze. "Just checking how deep it is, so I know what size to make the healing cord."

There were four cuts; one from each claw, but they weren't deep. I could make four small strips of cord rather than one wide, long one. It would take a little longer to do, but that would teach him not to backtalk my father.

I focused the Fae magic between my thumb and index finger, rubbing hard and fast, the warmth from the friction creating a yellow glow.

"Sinsra livris meris, sinsra livris meris, sinsra livris meris."

Andreas had already started a thread himself, so I stopped the process and all the power faded. I looked up at Father as an apprentice seeking advice from her master.

"What are you doing?" Father asked Andreas. "Athroxane must honour this to bless the Holy Fae Mother. It was her mistake."

"Relax, Trevor. I wasn't shaming her in front of our Fae Mother, I was just helping her along a bit, or this'll take longer than we have to spare. The other wild animals won't stay away forever and the longer we take to reach the Wolf Temple, the more likely it is that we arrive at a war zone."

Father grunted but didn't prohibit his actions any further.

I started again, Andreas mirroring my motions.

"Sinsra livris meris, sinsra livris meris, sinsra livris meris."

When my cord was the length of my finger, he focused his gaze on me.

"Ready?"

CHAPTER 5

He inhaled. "Together on three."

I panicked, shaking my head. "But won't that be more painful for you?"

His lips curled up to a half smile. "Yes, but less painful for you, Princess."

Behind me, Father grunted, but I didn't look.

I was his only heir, and I knew he wanted me to learn the tough lessons of life and not receive the cushy princess treatment. I needed to know how to rule Fairola Kingdom when that time came.

My mother had been a role model of a queen before she died. Everyone wanted to know, or be, Sandra Crawford, and it was a terrifying reputation to live up to. I hoped my father would never leave me in charge; he was better off training any of his commanders to become the next king than trying to shape me into a lady. I knew the laws and customs like the back of my hand but not because I'd studied them with great enthusiasm, no, only because I had been dragged through the boring ordeal; following in my father's footsteps. My passions were the treasure hunts for ancient artefacts, travelling the world and seeking out adventures. Like the one we'd just been on, but as all adventures, they come to an end and now it was time to return to the castle life and uphold my duties.

Andreas tapped my hand for attention. "So…together on three?"

I nodded at Andreas, arranging the cord by laying it straight in my palm, readying to press it against his bleeding wound.

Andreas raised his eyebrows at me. "One."

I placed my hand below the lowest cut.

"Two," he murmured as his neck compressed, and he looked down at his chest.

"Three," he called before screaming with his mouth closed as we both pressed the threads between the flaps of broken skin.

"Sinsra livris meris."

A flame ignited in my chest; a sensation like streaming fire gushed down my spine and legs, and it felt like someone had placed hot onyx along the length of my forearms.

"Sinsra livris meris," I called again.

My throat burned in my effort to force back the tears.

The closing wound finally dissolved the cord and the effects ebbed away. I panted hard to catch my breath, as I inspected the area. The cord had been strong enough to heal the skin together without leaving a visible mark.

I was relieved; I didn't want to use the painful magic more than necessary.

Andreas poked around with his fingers to inspect my work.

"Good job, Princess." He chuckled and winked at me. "Ready for the next go?"

I looked at the next wound, which was still oozing fresh blood. This wound was much larger.

I let out a sigh and nodded.

But before I put my fingers together, Vargo's voice rumbled behind me. "My King, let me heal Master Blackstorm in the princess's stead, so she can regain her strength."

Father started preparing to leave, threading on his shoulder bag and folding his arms into the straps of his quiver. "No! She must learn to be accountable for her own actions. Athroxane, again!"

I used my left hand this time to weave the cord, as my right-hand was still throbbing. The more I worked away on the cord, the fainter I felt.

Father walked up to me and handed me his water flask.

"You need to drink more."

I obeyed, as I didn't want to risk being marked with a brand line, although I had always wondered whether Father would actually punish me with one, or whether that might be the one time he turned a blind eye.

The water did help to wash down a lot of the discomfort in my throat.

I handed the flask back.

"I'm almost ready," I said, my voice muffled as I wiped my mouth with the back of my hand.

I rolled the glowing thread between my palms,

feeling it growing more potent as it thickened.

Andreas lifted his tunic once more. "Okay, I'll get naked."

He was a light-hearted man, but tough as steel. I wouldn't have been able to joke as much with that injury to my rib cage.

"You'll do the top one," he instructed, which was logical since his cord was bigger, but I was grateful that he had let me heal the smaller outer one. "One, two, three," he rumbled all at once before I was even properly prepared.

I hurried to stretch towards him so that we pressed the magic against his skin at the same time. At my squeak, Father shushed me. I knew it alerted all the wildlife in our location, but it couldn't be helped. The pain seared along my veins more intensely than the last go.

"Sinsra livris meris, sinsra livris meris, sinsra livris meris."

I felt like death by the time Andreas pulled his tunic down again.

"All done." He stood and went over to the cat. He heaved her up onto his shoulders, letting two legs hang down on either side of his neck. "Shall we?"

He carried on walking, crossing the gently flowing river.

Vargo fell into step behind me, tensely moving along and looking in every direction.

My white boots sloshed in the water as I jumped along some stepping stones with light steps.

On the other side of the spring, we continued onward, dry leaves and twigs crunching under our soles.

Vargo grabbed hold of my shoulder to halt me. I

was surprised as it wasn't far to the Wolf Temple from here. My father and Andreas also stopped.

"What is it?" I whispered.

No one answered, but they didn't have to. In the distance, there was a haunting cry, sounding like the last bellow before death, before an unnerving silence fell.

Father drew his sword, and Andreas followed. Vargo shuffled me behind him.

Out of the bushes in front of us, the bloodied form of Commander Detroy stumbled into view. Father raced to his side, supporting him under one shoulder.

"Commander, what happened to you?"

"The wolves, My King, they're slaughtering the platoon."

The Commander collapsed to the ground even though Father tried to break his fall.

"War," the Commander panted before his eyes closed and his body went limp.

CHAPTER 6

Father put his ear to the Commander's chest. "He's dead."

"He is also soaked," Andreas said. "There must be a storm up ahead."

Vargo turned to my father. "If there is a war and a big storm ahead, we should retreat back to the castle, my King."

If the Commander was in this state, the war must already be lost. Vargo knew it too, and so did my father. I observed my father, as he searched the Commander's body for any weapons he still had.

"Duty sometimes means death," my father said. "How can I ask my people to fight for me if I don't fight for them? I don't flee from my responsibilities."

"Neither does death flee from its responsibility," Andreas chided, obviously wanting Father to retreat in view of the bad odds. "To my better judgment though, you know I'll cover your back whatever you face. Lead on."

The battle code meant that Andreas must let Father take the lead, or else Andreas's vigour would have made him run to be the first man on the battlefield.

We ran into the greyer depths of the jungle where the swamp wet our boots and the hammering sound of heavy rainfall intensified, drowning out the clangs of crossing swords.

We were getting closer to the storm and there was only a short distance left until I would be faced with whatever was going on at the Wolf Temple. I pushed through the last part of the undergrowth, and the rain from the angry grey sky above us instantly soaked my hair and dress. The ground was trembling and a few tree roots had been torn from the soil and fallen over. The turmoil inside me instinctively screamed for me to turn around and go home and escape this horrible place.

The enormous temple stood tall in a raised clearing. Its massive flat roof was supported by hundreds of round pillars along its frame, and between them stood the ancient square temple building. There was a door there somewhere but you couldn't see it. Ivy climbed up its stone walls, finding any groove to hold on to and slithered all the way over the roof. There was a meadow all around it, upon which fighting soldiers were intent on murdering each other. The Fae were greatly outnumbered, dotting the field in scattered troupes, wearing black iron and red capes, while the wolves pressed in on them, in their silver armour and green capes.

What were the green capes doing here in Skyland territory? Those belonged to Alpha Wild Skully from the jungle district in the north? The Skyland wolf pack wore blue capes, not green. What had been said in that letter delivered to my father that had spurred this on?

Vargo pressed me down behind a boulder. "Prepare your bow with a blue cord, Princess. I'll hold off the enemy."

I fervently rubbed my fingers together, summoning blue magic.

"Sinsra livris meris, sinsra livris meris, sinsra livris meris."

When it was long enough, I wired it around an arrowhead. I peered up from my hideout to aim, but couldn't release, as the people were all muddled up in close combat.

As our guards saw Father and Andreas, they were like kittens arching their backs to become large mountain lions.

Suddenly, a cacophony of barks, howls and growls ruffled the serenity of the forest to my right. Out from the tree line ran hundreds of wolves, charging straight into the battle. I lifted my bow and arrow with the tangled blue cord once more, but then lowered it as I saw the wolves who had just arrived, were attacking Wild Skully's pack and not the Fae.

Clifford Moon, the Alpha of the Skyland City pack, walked out from the forest in human form, his gaze seeking out the Fae King. He looked annoyed, his black shoulder-length hair soaked by the rain, his silver suit stained with blood and mud, and probably smelling worse than wet dog.

When he saw my father in the dim light of the

early night, he started jogging up the hill towards the Wolf Temple shouting for him. "Fae King Crawford, take cover inside the temple!"

Father looked up, and without a second thought abandoned his opponent to follow Alpha Moon. Halfway up the hill, he turned to find Vargo and me.

"Bring Athroxane!" he yelled at Andreas who was standing only a short distance away.

Andreas's white hair swung from one shoulder to the other as he turned abruptly to race my way.

"You cover us," he instructed Vargo, yanking me to my feet.

Andreas curled my frame into his wide torso as we ran across the field and up the hill. Wounded guards screamed all around us while the blue essence of magic lingered like dust in the air.

The ground vibrated, creating small rifts, as if it wanted to get rid of us all, swallowing us up. I jumped over a small one to reach my father who wrenched me out of the way of a boulder rolling past that had been torn away from the temple's base. We approached the temple, looking for the way in, which door would open when the key, called the Wolf Eye, was inserted in a circular indentation in the wall. I pushed away the clustered ivy branches and searched my palms along the dank wall. I constantly had to look over my shoulder to ensure no one was about to attack me, as Vargo and Andreas had distanced themselves from me to help the others in the battle.

The earth shook, as a rockfall from the Wolf Temple cascaded down its high walls and Father pulled me away just before I would have been flattened to death. I thought my heart was going to punch a hole in my chest, it pounded so hard.

The rain battered my head and dripped down my forehead, hiding the tears on my face. Lightning struck and I cowered even tighter into my father's embrace. The thunder came next. I closed my eyes, my whole body was shivering.

"Father! Don't let me die!"

The ringing steel mixed with nature's wrath made it almost impossible to hear each other. The red sun setting in the west behind heavy black clouds was a constant reminder that time was ticking by.

"It's just a matter of time before Alpha Moon has it under control!" Father shouted, as he stroked his finger along the Wolf Temple's stone wall, looking for the keyhole.

Suddenly he stopped, and it looked like he had found it.

"Alpha Moon, toss the Wolf Eye to me!" he shouted over his shoulder.

I turned around to see the Alpha rushing up the sharply inclined landscape. I raced out to meet him halfway, so that he could return to the fight, but I tripped on a rock and my foot didn't follow on the same trajectory as the rest of me. Pain shot up my ankle as it twisted and my knees buckled under my weight, sending me tumbling down the hillside. I stopped as I slammed into a tree, the force sending me spinning on my stomach.

I lifted my head up towards the temple, spitting dead leaves from my mouth.

Damn it, I must get up! Roxie, you can do this!

I pushed myself to my knees. My father was waiting at the top of the hill. He still didn't seem to have the key from the Alpha that would enable him to open the door into the temple.

The ground shook once more, like a ship on rough seas, so I placed my hands either side of me on the soaking grass for balance.

The Fae Mother is angry!

More boulders tore from the temple structure together with the ivy that was trying to hold on to them, and viciously tumbled down its side, burying the temple's base. When rock hit rock, sparks flew sky-high in the air like angry fireflies.

My father was in the midst of it all. My heartbeat escalated the warning, as I saw Father fighting against Alpha Moon in the door opening.

Why are they fighting one another?

"Father! Move! Get out of there!"

Father managed to pull the Alpha dagger from Clifford's belt and stab his arm.

Red magic streamed around the bloodied dagger – a blood curse.

Holy Fae Mother. My heart stopped for a moment as I looked at the red essence seeking with its tendrils to fester on the Alpha.

"Father, what have you done!" I shouted and was on my way towards him when, in front of my eyes, a massive stone block fell to trap my father underneath.

I screamed and ran to him. His feet stuck out, and his upper body was lodged inside the temple. All the bones in his legs had been crushed. The rain was dancing with a relevé pitter patter in a pool of his blood that was seeping in forking rivers down the hill.

Andreas pulled me up by my waist and dragged me away.

"Athroxane! I'm sorry! We'll retreat!"

I didn't feel or see anything else. My mind was caught in a loop, playing my father's death on repeat.

Andreas towed me by the hand and I tried to keep up as fast as I could with my ailing ankle.

"Andreas! We can't leave the battlefield! We must return to fight!"

A swishing sound behind me ended with a thud and Vargo cried out.

"Don't look back, Princess. Just run!" Andreas barked and let go of my hand.

I didn't look back. I ran into the jungle, the stench of damp welcome as long as the treetops sheltered me from the rain. I sprinted faster than I ever knew I could, knowing that even if the wolves didn't catch up with me, I had no weapons on me to protect myself from the other dangers of the wild ahead.

I had lost sight of Andreas by the time I arrived at the Fae riverbank. The sounds around me stopped, leaving only an empty void like a well without water. I nestled myself into a large hollow tree trunk to hide and rest. I wrapped my arms around my knees, collapsed my forehead onto them and cried. Father's crushed legs were imprinted on my mind.

He's dead.

CHAPTER 7

My father was dead. Vargo was dead, and only the Holy Fae Mother knew where Andreas was. I was alone and cold, and I had no idea of where to place my next foot. The Fae Council would whisper shame over the royal name if I returned before the battle was won - returning otherwise was considered less than duty required. 'If I wasn't to die for my people, why should they die for me?' my father would have said.

But where could I go from here? I couldn't stay in the jungle long, I didn't possess the skills to survive. I sobbed against my red dress, feeling my corset dig into my hipbone. Everything was lost. Why had Wild Skully ventured out from the jungle territory, and why had father been fighting Alpha Moon with the Alpha dagger smothered in blood curse magic?

After my breathing had stabilised, I crawled out of

the tree trunk, listening for any threatening noises. If I could get to the outskirts of Fairola City, the greater the chances were that less rural Fae would recognise me without the court furs on; the contrasts were too extreme. I normally wore a black plaited wig over my milk white hair and large cloaks of fur concealed my delicate silk dresses. The only Fae alive who would recognise me were cook Clarence, the court members, Kerri and Andreas – if he was still alive. Possibly the Dungeon Master too from all the times I had played in the red tower chasing stray kittens. He had helped me rig the traps on occasions, but they never worked.

The hair rose on my arms as a chilly breeze swept by. It was becoming late and I wrapped my arms around my waist and started walking – where? I didn't know. Just closer towards my former home; a castle I would do almost anything right now to be able to return to, to curl into my soft bed and have Clarence bring me a mug of hot chocolate. But I was the person who was expected to stay in a battle until the very end, protecting every single Fae in my kingdom until the last man standing. No Fae would follow a leader who cowardly left a fight and if I went home and the people found out they would lynch me and hang me from the gallows.

I slept in the gutter of my own city that night, without a soul in the world caring for me. When I woke up in the morning, it seemed as if I was waking up to reality for the first time in my life. What I saw in front of me now was real life, experienced by less fortunate Fae.

My steps towards the small market were sly, as I hoped to avoid attention. The familiarity of Fae fashion embraced me like a mother's arms in comparison to what I had been through in the wolf territory. Dull coloured armour had been replaced by strongly dyed silks in all the shades under the sun. Jewellery adorned with gems dangled from all body parts, from the top of Fae's long pointy ears to their small delicate toes tucked into open plaited sandals.

I looked at my dirty white boots, ruined beyond recognition. My red dress was blood stained and torn. I resembled a beggar, which was the polar opposite of whom I had always been.

I walked between the stalls, listening to the friendly gossip between neighbours. Glowers were tossed my way occasionally, pinning me as a stranger. I touched my aching stomach, as I noted a cherry which had fallen off the fruit trader's table and was lying on the ground. I almost felt the urge to stoop so low as to eat it, but even if I did, one cherry would be like dropping a pebble into the jaw of a giant gorge. I needed a job before I would see a decent meal.

What could I do?

I was good at needlework after countless hours under Maid Marciela's watch, and I was good at sparring with my sword and aiming with my bow, but it didn't appear as if someone would hire a young woman to do a man's job around here.

At the far end of the rows there was a market stall piled high with bolts of fabric and a large woman stood next to it, shouting out her prices. I headed for the stall. On my way, I stopped by another table, displaying artefacts.

Joyful butterflies entered my stomach as I eyed the beauties, but I had to shrug back as my eyes worked their way up to gaze upon the seller. He was grotesque with a red fleshy scar next to his left eye, which the crow sitting on his shoulder was trying to pick away at every now and again. His long hair cascaded all the way to the ground along a one-piece brown robe and a wolf-fur cape.

I forced my gaze away from the man and down onto the table again. Now I noticed that there were wonders of treasures mixed in with adeptly made replicas of real artefacts. I recognised in the work, many of the artisans who were being copied from what Father had taught me during our treasure hunts and from having grown up in his treasure chambers in the castle.

As I was admiring the pieces, a gentleman approached the table gauging the gold and glitters. He wore a gold headband clad with gems that pressed his hair to his head. Long transparent stones hung from his ears and gold decorated the hem of his long ocean-blue cape. He wore black leather gloves that had a ribbed pattern which coordinated perfectly with his tall boots. The gold belt that was squeezed tight around his waist held his posture fully erect.

The seller, who had ignored me, jumped off his chair, putting down a tiara he had been polishing until it was able to outshine the sun.

"Feast your eyes on these treasures of the world. The bracelet of Gwenda the Grim, the Captain's Dagger from the first ever voyage to Qualmar, and the never before available for sale amulet of our late Fae Queen."

Grief entered my soul when the seller referred to my mother. I was the reason for her death at childbirth. I'd never known her but the seller might have known of her. Although, what I did know was that the amulet was fake. The original lay in the larger drawer in my jewellery-box and even if I'd never seen it before in my life, my trained eye wouldn't be fooled by this replica. Blacksmith Fromier, who the Royal family employed, would never in his wildest dreams cut corners to present such shoddy workmanship.

The rich Fae only gave a brief and discontented grunt in reply to the tradesman who didn't seem to have done a day's honest work in his life; nor had he probably given a genuine smile that wasn't from greed or gloat.

The rich Fae cleared his throat. "I need a present for a young lady..." He turned to look at me. "Roughly your age, I would say. Which one would you choose?"

I looked down at the items on the table, contemplating my answer.

"The amulet."

I had advised him of the worst option with a plan in mind. If one couldn't afford to be honest, I might as well be a thief to survive. The emptiness in both my stomach and my heart made the decision easier.

"I'll have it then," he said with glee, handing over payment and sliding the necklace containing the amulet down into his coat pocket.

He lifted his hat at me in thanks before strolling down the market street. The seller tossed the coins in his palm.

"You have a keen eye to spot beauty," he marvelled in his lucrative heist.

I snorted. "Keen enough to see that it was a fake."

The coins stopped flat in his hand.

"Nonsense!" He huffed, looking around nervously to assess whether anyone had heard me.

I pointed at more counterfeit goods. "And that

one, and that one, and the goblet at the end."

Evil entered his eyes, and without warning, the man pulled his knife from his waistband and swung it straight for me.

CHAPTER 8

He slammed it towards my hand on the table. Had I not retracted it in time, he would have cut it clean off. I dug my heels into the ground to race away, but the man caught my wrist, restraining my freedom. I started hyperventilating in panic, tears filling my lower eyelids.

"No! Let go of me!" I didn't recognise my own high-pitched voice with so much fright stuck in my throat.

The merchant dragged me kicking and screaming to the private part of his tent, his grip so hard it was going to leave me bruised.

"Be quiet, or I'll cut your throat," he hissed, holding the large blade against my neck.

"Yes, that's not fake," I whimpered.

He didn't appreciate the irony, pressing the blade harder against me. I squealed.

"I'll not have you ruin my business, you Fae bitch!"

He was flexing his muscles, ready to slice me.

"I won't! I told him to get the fake! I helped you!"

He hesitated.

I only took shallow breaths.

"Hmm. You could be useful to me."

"I know a lot about artefacts. I'll work for a small fee."

"Payment?" He chuckled ruefully. "No you should be grateful you're alive. That's your payment. I actually do need someone to retrieve the North Fairola Temple Script for me."

I gasped. "Steal from the temple?"

The man pressed the blade to my skin. "You'd rather I stole your life?"

I gave a tight shake of my head, afraid to move too much against his dagger.

"I'll do it if I can get an advance. I'm so hungry, I don't think I'll succeed in getting it for you unless I'm fed first."

"You're homeless?"

"Yes."

His eyebrows creased. "Your parents?"

I shook my head.

"So, how come you know so much?"

"Growing up on the streets, you know, picked up a few tricks."

"You didn't grow up on the streets. You're lying to me. No beggar could afford the dress you're wearing."

"I stole it," I hastened to say, as the cold steel closed in on my skin.

"Well," he said, inspecting me from top to toe. "You can't need much in that tiny belly."

He let go of me and went to his desk which was buried under jewels and paperwork. With a sharp lead pencil he scribbled a short line on a note before handing it to me.

"Show this to one of the two guards stationed outside the gates of Chateau Fae Crow."

I read the message on the note. 'A new apprentice.' It was signed, 'Master Crowland'.

So this was Master Crowland. I had heard so much about him, but hoped I would never meet him. Now, I was caught in his web of spiders, a fate worse than a royal exile.

A knot twisted in my gut; I was in such deep trouble.

I had heard of the heavily fortified castle on the north-western hills and I had also heard that no one entered voluntarily. Many traders had been invited there for negotiations and none of them had ever come back out – unless they had agreed to his terms. But, what had happened to them couldn't be worse than dying of hunger or being beheaded by the council, could it?

I had a strong feeling I would regret this decision. In a place like Crowland's, you were trained and formed to become whatever they needed you to be; con-artists, thieves or even murderers.

"You look like a dumb donkey standing here loitering over my precious goods. Off with you," he boomed. "Make me a rich man, or I'll cut my losses."

I reflexively protected my throat with my hand as he let go of me, stroking my unbloodied skin to ensure it was still untouched by his blade.

Master Crowland chuckled darkly. "Don't worry, I start with the ears and work my way down to the throat. And don't even think of running. You're mine now. You wouldn't want to look over your shoulder for the rest of your life to protect that pretty face of yours."

I touched my ear. I very much wanted to keep my ears, so I turned around and ran as if a wolf was hunting me, snapping its teeth at my heels.

My sprint soon ebbed off to a jog and later a stumbling walk before I reached my new Master's holdfast. It was still only morning, but the sun that made the wildflowers stretch tall like a pink blanket over the rolling hills didn't seem to reach all the way to the castle. As if unable to absorb beauty, the castle had allied itself with the few clouds there were in the sky to maintain in an eerie shadow where evil could develop. I could imagine monsters who dwelt there, jumping out from behind the giant fangs and claws of the gargoyles.

I wanted to fall to my knees and crawl to the nearest standing guard. It was so intimidating how I could only see his eyes from below a hollowed out white lion-head. The teeth of which decorated the guard's forehead, and the paws of which clad his shoulders. Between these, a red scarf was pulled up just above his nose. Below, a white fur with plaited ropes hung from his hips and decorated the edges of his black armoured chest plate, handguards and knee boots. The bizarre outfit made the hairs on my arms stand up.

I handed the guard my note and he instantly tapped his spear on the ground twice, which made the other larger guard move two paces forward to be ready to hold the fort in his stead. Like a well-disciplined warrior, the pale face turned a sharp sideways angle to align with the fence, and pushed the iron gate open to let me in - or lock me up, depending on how you looked at it.

I could almost feel the tip of the spearhead poking my back as I crossed the front yard towards the stone building, which had more towers than I had fingers and more chambers than I had bones in my body.

Instead of entering the front door, he ushered me around the back of an inner ward where a doorless opening in the castle wall was ready to swallow me whole. Inside it was dark, with only a few fire-lit torches to lead our way. I breathed slowly but my heart tapped away to continuously remind me of my stupidity. We carried on down some winding stairs. The dungeon felt as if it was closing in on me. My breathing started to echo and I heard grains of sand scrape under the soles of my feet with every step I took. As we descended, the air became heavier to breathe and it caressed a raw chill along my bare arms. Despite how much I hated to wear the court furs, right now they would have been appreciated.

The guard stopped. "Do you prefer a room in the front, or at the back?"

"A room. Here?"

I looked down the length of a deep corridor to see prison cells line both sides of the passageway.

What have I gotten myself into?

CHAPTER 9

I peered into the first cell. There were only three stone walls and a bed pressed against one of them.

"Any of the back rooms have four walls or a window?"

The guard snorted, amused. "Aren't you a princess locked up for the first time."

My heart sank. He hadn't meant it literally, he was mocking me. If he only knew how right he was.

"Can I see the other rooms?"

He laughed, bending over. "This isn't an inn, it's where we keep our workers stacked for counting. They all look the same, kid."

"Then this one is fine." I sighed, feeling all my life draining within a deep sigh.

"Welcome to your new home then," he said with a merry hand gesture for me to enter. "I'll have the cook bring food."

I slumped down on the hard bed, but flew back up as the guard left without locking the gate.

Why has he not secured me in here? I thought I was a prisoner.

I sprinted after the guard towards the unclosed gap between the bars leading out.

"Aren't you going to lock the door?"

"The cells lock at midnight when we take stock. If you aren't accounted for, you'll be found and cut." The guard hadn't even stopped or turned to look my way as he answered.

This was a nightmare. The prisoners were so disciplined, or scared to death, that they didn't even dare fleeing with their cell doors wide open. As the guard had intimated, I was one of Master Crowland's possessions now and no longer a person in my own right.

I wonder how many more he owns.

I turned my head the other way to listen if there were more of us here. I couldn't hear any voices, but perhaps they were all out on missions to plunder and pillage. I pressed my palms to squeeze my face together from the agony, thinking of my future life, until I heard a clattering that sounded like clay dishes and cutlery on a tray. I opened my eyes, eagerly awaiting my lunch like a stray cat would when expecting someone to throw it leftovers.

My eyes almost popped out of their sockets when I saw the wide woman in her customary green dress, fastened with a large golden belt at her waist.

I darted for her. "Clarence!"

She shoved the sharp edge of the tray straight into my chest, sending me tumbling backwards.

What the Demon Dogs!

She sneered at me; a malicious smile curling her lips on both ends. "They said you were dead."

Fear burned in my gut. Her tone of voice when speaking to me had completely changed.

What had happened to her? Her brown frizzy hair was trapped into three iron rings, making her gleaming green eyes full of hatred, the focal point on her chubby face.

I crawled backwards like a crab and up onto my bed. "Please, don't tell anyone that I'm alive."

"Don't worry about that, Doll. I'll enjoy seeing you suffer a long and horrible death. But if you give me grief, I might change my mind."

Without bending, Clarence dropped the tray to the floor so that the glass tipped water into the white lumpy mess filling a clay bowl. I quickly ran and glided on my knees towards it so as to try and salvage what I could.

Clarence's wicked laughter bounced on the walls. She was obviously amused at seeing me crawl on my knees for scraps.

I looked up at her. "Why are you doing this to me?"

"Sorry Doll, I work for Master Crowland full-time now. This has been my home during the hours I wasn't working in the castle and I didn't bother to go to the castle today after hearing rumours of your death. I only wish the rumours had been true, you made my life a living hell."

"But, but...we had fun. You tickled me. You fed me. I considered you my Nana."

She tilted her head, putting on a fake pouting face. "Aww. Have I broken your gold plated heart?"

"Yeah, well, you've made a crack in it."

Her expression changed; it now wore a hue of remorse. Irked, she turned her saggy black boots around and stormed off.

I can't flipping believe this.

I stared at the tray of food with aching knees and a bleeding heart. The porridge in the bowl had turned into a sloppy mess from all the water spilt into it and it tasted like Merry Kerri's attempt at baking oat biscuits which always lacked enough sugar.

I thought about my chambermaid and I wondered what had happened to her now that I was assumed dead. But I was sure she was going to thrive at anything she did. She wasn't called Merry Kerri for no reason; no one could bring her mood down, her presence brought out sunshine even at night. She always turned my gloomy mood right round whatever was the matter. Unless, her friendship was also fictitious, like Clarence's had proven to be.

Before I had even finished my food, the guard came back, thumping a wooden crate on the floor next to me.

He looked down at me, the jaw of the wild skin hood towering menacingly over me. "You're accounted for. Get to work."

I craned my neck to peek inside the box, curious as to its contents, as only the hilt of a sword handle poked above the edge. There was black fabric and more iron inside.

I took another spoonful of my sloppy porridge. "I'll start tomorrow at first light." My commanding princess tone not amiss.

The guard didn't hesitate to draw a thin rod with an attached metal piece from its sheath, which hung next to his sword on his belt.

What the heck is that?
Not that it mattered, I didn't want to get anywhere near it.

CHAPTER 10

I wasn't more than a second away from pulling the sword from the crate and parrying his first strike. My arm trembled as the sword was heavy enough for a strong man. My own sword would only measure half of its length.

The man smiled, obviously impressed. "You start when I say you start, Crowlander."

"I'm not a Crowlander!"

He pushed the tip of the rod onto my skin just below my shoulder. It burned like when I accidentally touched Clarence's baking trays when stealing freshly baked biscuits. He removed it and I looked at my angered red skin.

He laughed darkly. "Now you are."

Ahhh! My royal fae skin!

On my arm, a black crow marked my skin – a symbol that I belonged to his fellowship.

"Don't be upset Twiggy, you will die before long, anyway."

I was angering to the point that my blood boiled. "Are you coming with me?"

"No!" He snorted patronisingly.

"Then get out of my face!"

His superior smile dropped, and he said nothing, walking off.

I hovered over the wooden crate, inspecting my options and picked up the black soft leather that turned out to be a one piece suit. I changed into it, lacing it all the way to my chin and buckled on the holster straps around my legs, shoving into them as many knives as I could fit. Other than those, I planned to travel lightly; no sword or bow and arrow this time. The contract required me to be inconspicuous like a shadow and soundless as a hunting wild cat. If I was caught stealing a Fae Mother scroll, my life would be over without a doubt; and the Fae Mother would curse my afterlife.

I cut off a piece of the thin rope I found rolled up at the bottom of the crate to tie up my hair. Ready for thieving one of the four most sacred artefacts in Fae history, I jogged out of the dungeon and towards the gates. The guards held them open for me, keeping their expressions stoic and unfriendly.

"Be back before midnight," the second guard announced robotically, as if he had been instructed to repeat those orders every time someone left the castle grounds.

My tactic had to be aced. I couldn't exhaust myself too soon in the quest but also I had to push hard enough so as not to miss my curfew either. I started jogging at a comfortable pace; every thumping heartbeat reminded me that I had less time.

When I reached the road leading down to the North Fae Temple, I got off it to hide in the dense overgrowth. I took a break to rest, drink from a rain-filled leaf and eat some nuts and berries. I rushed it, since this time I didn't have the protection of three strong men, should a wild animal cross my path. I stayed low to the ground, creeping closer, observing the area.

Two guards were patrolling the top landing of the temple but none seemed to be stationed at the ground. I watched them for a while. They seemed to be walking round and round the landing on opposite ends, but they were not well synchronised, leaving a brief moment before both had a view on the front side.

I could make that sprint.

The timing had to be perfect. It couldn't take longer than holding in one breath. I hesitated. If I went through with this, I would never feel the same way about myself again and if I was caught and recognised, they would bring me to the court to be executed, but if I didn't steal the script and wasn't back to Master Crowland before midnight they'd cut my throat. There was a lot at stake and there seemed to be no way out of my misery so I took a deep breath, waited until the guards went around the corner and then darted across the field to the temple. I reached the front to hide under the roof, pressing myself up tight against the wall.

No alarms were raised and I breathed heavily before sidling along the cold stone wall towards the doors. Carefully, I leaned across the open doors to have a look inside. My heart pounded like a whole gnu stampede.

The temple was empty of Fae from what I could see, but the holy building was big, so that wasn't necessarily the case. My first target was the back row of pews and I hunched down; abs crunched over, keeping low on my knees as I hid. On hands and feet, I moved like a gracious wolf closer to the altar.

I looked around, still seeing no one. The script was kept in a gold cylinder in the hands of the Fae Mother sculpture on the wall above the altar. In plain sight. Good for detecting but not so much for stealing unnoticed. I took a deep determined breath, tasting the spicy incense that swirled into my mouth. The temple master had lit them so it meant he must be around here somewhere and I made sure I inspected all areas of the hall. The frescos were to the same scale as the living Fae, easily camouflaging someone who stood close to admire them.

I couldn't see anyone moving nor could I hear any noises except for the crickets singing outside. The temple was as quiet as a grave ten feet under the soil. I tucked my head into my chest, praying to the Fae Mother for forgiveness. I was so ashamed for what I must do, but it was this or die.

I took the two steps up to the altar table and twirled quickly to sit behind it. All I needed to do now was get off the cold floor and grab the scroll.

Then run.

I stretched up on my toes, my knees shaking, curving my fingers around the gold cylinder. I yanked it out of the Fae Mother's giving hands. A waft of dust and metal hit my nostrils and I felt the embossed flowery pattern on the cylinder. It was sharp to hold, grinding uncontrollably at my blisters, but I had the artefact and now I only needed to get back to Crowland before midnight.

I fastened the scroll into the belt around my leg before sprinting for the door, but I had abruptly to skid to a halt in the doorway.

Shit!

Four men were dismounting their horses just outside the temple. I hadn't heard them arrive. The tension must have blocked out the clop of their horses's hooves.

I peered out again. They were coming this way. I searched their hands and arms with a quick glance. No one was holding anything that looked dead or newly born needing to be blessed, that might indicate the reason they'd come to the temple. I leaned back inside, pressing my back up against the wall.

Why were they here?

What to do now?

If I took them by surprise, I could probably dash past them without them noticing the scroll.

I waited for the moment they were just outside the doors with my heart drumming for war. I took deep breaths and counted my rhythm with a children's rhyme which ironically Clarence used to keep telling me. "What should the Fae who meets a wolf say; run away, run away!"

I aimed for the gap in-between two of the big blokes and launched myself forwards. I pushed past and went flying down the steps, two at a time, feeling the sting that was still festering in my twisted ankle.

I didn't look back but could hear the disgruntled snorts of the offended men; that was until they realised that I was stealing one of their horses. Then they got a bit more fire under their boots, but didn't manage to reach me before I had swung up onto the horse and was galloping down the grassy slope.

Not hearing any hooves pursuing me, I glanced back over my shoulder.

It can't have been that easy.

The two guards at the battlement were leaning over the wall, shouting something incomprehensible and below them, I saw the other horses still bound to a rail by the temple. Then I heard growls just behind me – four large wolves were at both my flanks, catching up with the horse.

They weren't Fae, they were wolf shifters! I had stolen a horse from a wolf shifter! What were they doing on Fae territory?

I kicked my heels into the horse; panicking from the fear of death by a sharp jaw digging into my arteries. I did not want to die being mauled by wolves.

Inevitably, they quickly caught up with my new speed, snapping their teeth at the horse's hind legs. I urged the horse on harder. Mazzi would have been faster than this one, but she was still somewhere in the wolf district, unless they'd already killed her.

Another wolf suddenly appeared out of the woods from the side, stopping right in front of the horse, barking menacingly. Frightened, the horse reared, neighing wildly and I was flung off its back, hitting the ground with a thud. Pain seared through me, but I needed to get up and run, although, I knew the odds; who, on two legs, could outrun five wolves?

CHAPTER 11

I didn't even get up on my knees before five large wolf heads hovered above mine. Instinctively, I drew my knives from the leg holsters, holding them up, ready to stab the first one who flinched.

The one at my feet seemed eager, but my eyes were focused on the largest grey and white speckled one to my right, whose bite would be fatal. They spat their saliva at me as they barked, their wolf breath stinking of recently eaten corpses. The largest wolf who had come out from the woods, let out a single final bark and the other four wolves vanished down the road.

What had just happened? Why were they leaving? The remaining wolf seemed to be waiting for something to happen. He was staring up at the crescent moon that illuminated the late evening.

Suddenly, he shifted to his human form, but all I

could see was firm buttocks and brown hair down to his shoulders. He immediately went over to the horse who was grazing nearby, grabbing hold of its reins. He showed it affection by stroking along its neck before digging some clothes out of one of the saddlebags.

My instincts told me to make a run for it as he had his back towards me, but his tranquil manner made me too curious. Besides, even on two legs, he looked muscular enough to outrun me. My forced breathing had started to subdue by the time the man had finished pulling on a beige shirt and white linen trousers. When he turned to face me, I recognised him. I wasn't out of danger yet!

"Blake Moon?" It was the Skyland Alpha heir; at a Fae Temple.

"Good evening, Princess."

I put my hands behind my back, hoping he wouldn't notice I had started on a blue magic cord. "You must have me confused; I'm not a princess."

With determined strides he approached, squatted down in front of me and held my chin between his thumb and index finger. "A fairer face, I have never seen." He let go and stood up, looking down on me. "I was looking for you."

Oh no, I didn't want to be dragged back to the Fae castle, but neither did I want to be a wolf shifter hostage. But who was I kidding? Maybe he was not holding me as hostage and was just going to kill me and be done with it. I rubbed faster at the blue cord.

Sinsra livris meris, Sinsra livris meris, Sinsra livris meris!

"I wanted to ask a favour of you."

"What?" I felt stumped; my hands halting their weaving process. "What did you say?"

His thin lips smiled into a line and his green eyes glinted like the stars in the sky. "Please, can you get up on the horse again?"

Oh, that favour; to be a good hostage.

"You are mocking me."

He cocked his head from one side to the other. "A little bit."

He was a handsome man. Had he been a Fae, I may have gladly gone with him.

"I'll scream."

Blake waved his arms. "Go ahead, Princess. Maybe the guards will come to escort you back to the palace."

He knew! He was accustomed to the Fae traditions and was either bluffing or there had been some developments at the castle to suggest my death or my deceit. I couldn't go back; they'd shame my family and execute me and I didn't want to have my head severed from my shoulders, I quite liked them being attached. My lovely face wouldn't fashion well, being spiked on a spear and flagged as that of a coward at the city gates.

"What do you want from me?"

"I want you to get up on the horse with me."

"With you?"

"Yeah, I'm not going to walk."

I rubbed my forehead. I saw no way out of this; if I ran, he would just shift and come after me.

I stood up, keeping my hand behind my back.

He sighed before walking back to the saddlebag, bringing out a thin rope. "I didn't want to do this; toss all your knives out of reach and hold your hands out."

I needed to be quick, I had to spiral the blue cord

around the knife I held in my hand and jab it into Blake's flesh for it to be absorbed by his blood. That was a tall order to manage when he stood only a short distance away, but simply pressing it for a brief moment onto his skin wasn't going to do much damage.

I hesitated for a moment, but realised that it had to be now as I couldn't hide away the knife and cord in my one-piece overall.

I didn't attack. Why couldn't I bring myself to attack him?

"Fine," I blurted out, tossing the cord on the ground where it dissolved when devoid of its feeding energy source. I held my hands in front of him with my wrists aligned. "Not so hard."

He wore an amused smirk on his face as he started to wrap the rope around my wrists. He finished by tying a weak double loop which wouldn't hold a sheep. I couldn't be sure whether to take it as an insult or as him being merciful.

I stretched out my arms to display his own handy work close to his face. "So, how do I get up on the horse now?"

"By standing on that rock." Blake pointed at a knee-high boulder.

"I still won't be tall enough to swing my leg over the saddle."

"I'll lift you the rest of the way. Now, get up on it, and please, don't try to run, we both know how that will end."

The way his smooth voice rolled out the warning made the tip of my ears burn. He was quite a charming man. He circled the horse around my way before I had even contemplated getting up on the rock. He mounted and clicked with his tongue for the horse to move. It was a lovely stallion; black in colour with a shine to its coat, and with Blake on top, the two of them looked like a vision of my childhood daydreams where a prince used to come calling at my balcony to offer his loyal service.

He suddenly brought me out of my thoughts. "Do you want me to help you up onto the rock too?"

"No," I stretched the word to highlight his patronising remark.

I rocketed away, jumping up onto the rock with just one step and without using my hands.

He again showed his charming smile without offering a comment, but I thought he looked impressed. That smile was getting to be annoying or confusing, as it made me feel both insulted and warm inside.

He aligned the stallion with its flank against the rock. "Turn around, Princess."

I wasn't sure what he was playing at, but did as I was bid. Not long after, I felt his arms hook under my armpits, lifting me up effortlessly to sit sideways in front of him.

"Swing your leg over."

With a grunt, I leaned back, hitting his hard chest as I awkwardly folded my leg over the horse's neck. Blake cradled me between his arms, holding onto the reins on either side of me. He made a forwards rolling motion with his hip and that made the horse trot. His crotch had rubbed against my back, also managing to make my privates tingle.

What was wrong with me? He is my enemy. His father just killed mine.

I scratched at my lap, pretending to alleviate an

itch running down my leg. In the darkness maybe he wouldn't notice me grabbing for the knife in my boot.

Swiftly, I pulled the tiny hilt from my boot and swirled it around, wedging the blade so it was hidden between my loosely bound wrists. Blake didn't seem to have noticed but weirdly, he seemed to be sniffing gently at my hair. Occupied with his focus at my neck, I glanced down at his thigh, looking for a good spot to strike. His arms were bobbing in rhythm with the trot, and were holding me too firmly to allow me to get any leeway or gain momentum for the stab.

His warm breath enveloped my ear. "I wouldn't do that if I were you."

My breathing stiffened. How could he have noticed?

"And what had you planned to do after you had planted the knife in my leg?"

CHAPTER 12

"Push you off the horse and ride home?"

Warm laughter repeated in my ear. "And where is your home, nowadays?"

A pang of something like desolation beat in my chest. I had no home. Only a rat-infested crawl-inn and a flea stuffed bed in Crowlands's dungeon.

"That blow was below the belt."

"You were going to stab me and push me off my horse! I call it even."

His calm behaviour made no sense and he still made no effort to remove my weapon. What did he want with me?

We rode in silence for a long while, until I felt his crotch starting to stir in the saddle.

"The sun is coming up; we should make camp and rest."

"I can't sleep now; it's morning. Fae sleep at

night."

"Sorry that your beauty sleep is mixed up, Princess. You can continue towards Skyland City if you like and I can catch up."

Confused, I raised my brows. "You're telling your prisoner to ride to her captivity on her own?"

"You are not a prisoner. I told you, I only want to ask a favour of you."

"You don't have to take me all the way to Skyland City, ask me now."

"I want you to get to know me better first, in the hope you won't say no."

"So, this is how you believe you are going to impress me?" I raised my bound hands to demonstrate my lack of free choice.

"If I hadn't, I would have been dead by now. Your reputation extends to my throne room equally as to yours."

There was some truth in that, I supposed. If he wanted to wine and dine me, he had to start by tying me up, or I would fight for my freedom.

We hadn't even halted when I felt Blake swing down from the horse. "I trust you know the way?"

The horse stopped and I stared down at his kind green eyes. It made my anger rise.

"And what if I turn back?"

This was so strange.

"I'm already going to ask you for one favour, don't make me ask for another of you; I'm not the begging type."

He smacked the horse's rear. It started into a canter and I twisted in the saddle to see the distance between us grow.

I hurriedly tore my hands out of the rope and

shook it off so that it landed on the ground. I gripped hard on the reins and yanked them to make the horse circle around. I had made no promises to the wolf; I had to get back to Crowland before they noticed I was missing at midnight. Right now, I wished I hadn't chosen the first cell, but it was better to lose an ear than my life.

I only managed to turn around before the path was blocked by four furry legs. I sighed, seeing Blake watching me with his wolf eyes. I forced the horse in an arc to get around him, but he just looped sideways, herding the horse back on track like a sheepdog.

"I thought you said you were going to rest," I blurted out.

He responded with a loud bark.

"Fine!"

I turned the horse towards Skyland City as my predicament sunk in. Blake wasn't going to let me off the hook, he was going to drag me to the feet of my father's killer one way or another, and the Crowland crew were going to keep hunting me until they'd cut me up, piece by piece.

I had never been to Skyland City, but I didn't need to know the way, Blake was quick to correct any misstep to bring the horse back onto the right path. I thought he would soon scare the life out of the poor thing if he carried on like that. Maybe I could get it to kick out and rid us of our captor; one hoof square in the face should do it. He had quite a handsome face when he was human though and it would be a shame to ruin it.

I dropped the thought and carried on. Leafy branches scraped against my legs and I had to bend around a few that closed in on my face. I felt exhausted from not having slept all night; if I had been relaxed enough, I would have collapsed on the horse's back. I spotted a waterhole to my left and decided to stop for a rest. Blake seemed to think it was a good idea too, as he didn't bark at me for dismounting and leading the stallion to have a drink.

I could let go of its reins because Blake wasn't going to let it go, unless I smacked its rear and made it gallop off. But that probably just meant that he would let it run and I would have to walk the rest of the way – so not a great plan.

The moss under my soles was soft, making my tired feet bounce as I stepped. I bent down to feel it but determined that it wasn't dry enough to sit on.

Blake's bark startled me. I looked up and saw him nodding at the horse's flank where a blanket was rolled up and strapped behind one of the side saddlebags.

I crossed my arms disdainfully, but then let out a frustrated roar. I didn't want his help, but I was extremely tired and I stomped towards the horse and started untying the blanket. The animal didn't even flinch and just kept drinking. It must have been so thirsty.

I spread the furry blanket out on top of the moss where its underside made of skin kept the wet from soaking through and I actually lay down, tucking my hands under my cheek. It was heavenly. It must have been even softer than my own bed.

My not-so-hostile travelling companion lay down on his tummy a short distance away, licking his front paws. He was constantly on guard, his eyes twitching between the forest around us and me, while his ears flicked in every direction. I almost felt it would serve him right if a baboon showed up. Not that I wanted to fight one myself if any did jump us.

Even though I was fighting sleep, my eyes were getting heavy. I tried my hardest to keep myself awake but the tiredness numbed my focus and soon, I felt that black lulling comfort behind closed eyelids wrapping around me. Had I not felt so safe in Blake's care, I would have sat up, but he needed me for something important and wasn't going to allow me to die from the sharp teeth of any hungry predator in the forest – not yet.

A restful night was what I firmly believed I would have until a warm hand on my shoulder shook me wildly.

CHAPTER 13

Blake's chest was too close to my face as I opened my eyes, for me to understand what I was looking at, at first. His torso looked like a mountain landscape with rounded tops and rippling gorges.

He was in human form?

"Wake up! You don't need any beauty sleep."

And was the dog complimenting me on my beauty now?

I sat up abruptly, almost knocking foreheads in the darkness surrounding us. I looked around and couldn't see the horse at the water hole but then detected it grazing just a short distance away. The entire situation confused me.

Why has he woken me up in the middle of the night?

The heavens were black and the stars dotted the sky. I looked up at Blake who was still kneeling down next to me, his deep green eyes focused on my reaction.

"It's night. Why did you wake me up?" I hardly believed it was my turn to keep watch.

His black leather trousers squeaked when he straightened his legs. "I want to sneak into Skyland Castle as undetected as possible. You know…all the Alpha heir fame…and you being the Fae princess."

"You mean that you don't want anyone to know you've kidnapped me?"

"Here we go again."

I fumed when I saw him rolling his eyes at me. No one dared to do that to a member of the royal family in the Fairola Kingdom.

He looked up at the moon. "What's the likelihood of you trusting someone you barely know?"

"A Fae; a hundred percent, a wolf; zero."

"And a human shifter?" he added with a charming smile.

I glowered at him menacingly. "You're still a dog."

He took a deep breath and cocked his head. "Is a dog better or worse than a wolf?"

"Ugh!" I flew to my feet, stomping off towards the horse.

I heard him chuckling behind my back and saw him roll up the furred skin as I looked over my shoulder.

More infuriating was that the horse was too tall, so I needed help to get up and looking around, I couldn't see a bloody stone anywhere to use as a step. I'd rather walk the horse back to Skyland City than ask Blake for assistance. I looked back at him and saw that smirk that he must have perfected a long time ago. It was flawless and could irritate the calm out of the Fae Mother.

"Put that smirk away, or I'll stitch those lips shut when I next get the chance!"

He relaxed them into a deliberate pout. "Need any help there, Princess?"

He was eyeing me and the horse, obviously realising my dilemma.

"Urg! No! Well...yes, but no. I can do it myself."

He chuckled some more, leaning back against a tree, crossing his feet at his ankles as he kept on watching me.

I held the reins out to him. "It's your turn to ride, anyway. I'll walk."

He pushed away from the trunk, walking over to grab the reins without a word, only a twitching mouth which was trying to hide his smirk. He swung up effortlessly, stretching down a hand towards me.

"We can both ride, if you promise not to stab me in the leg."

I thought for a moment before I clasped his arm and was immediately suspended into the air and over the horse's neck.

"I make no promises to a wolf," I muttered.

Agony deriving from unwanted desire slithered around in my stomach, like I'd eaten a dozen yellow magic cords, when he enveloped his arms around me.

Thank the Fae Mother, I'm not sitting behind him, gripping around his naked chest.

Blake was sniffing my hair next to my ear again. "Your body heat has risen."

Now I thought that I could really hear the smirk in his voice.

"Well...it's a warm night."

"I'd say it's rather cool."

I flapped my hands. "Well, your body is hot."

"Thank you!"

"Knock it off! I didn't mean it that way. I mean, your wolf body temperature is warming against my back."

"Sure," he said, the little word still loaded with sarcasm.

"Mention it again and I'll put some power behind a blue magic cord and jam it into your pants."

"Ouch! That would totally cripple my pride pillar."

"It won't be much more than a droopy dipper after that, so zip it if you want to keep your pride."

"Of course, Milady!"

His humour did amuse me, even though I tried my best to ensure he knew his kind was my enemy but a twitch by the side of my lip threatened to curl and reveal a smile. I sighed deeply, looking up at the sky. A sinister glow of yellow, shading into green, became more prominent the further we cantered forwards and I could only assume we were approaching the Skyland City. My heart started pounding. Soon, I would be without any means to escape. If I entered beyond the city walls, I doubted I would ever make it out again. The only thing that could save me was a collaboration, regarding to this 'favour' that Blake had mentioned. But what favour could be so special that the wolves needed me? If Alpha Moon was contemplating a Fae princess for an in-law, he could bloody forget it. I'd rather hang from the gallows or have my head spiked and flagged from their gatehouse before I promised the Fae Mother that I'd bind myself to Blake.

I was beginning to think that our ride was never going to end along this path, when I finally saw the last row of trees and beyond that a broad field. Blake pulled the reins to slow the horse to a walk. The last leafy branch slapped against my face before we were free of the jungle; a slap that felt like that of the Fae Mother, beating the disbelief out of me. My eyes looked upwards, following along the walls of tall buildings that never seemed to end. This type of architecture was unheard of in the Fae territory. A multitude of thin towering pillars with sharp peaking formations soared to the sky, impaling the clouds.

No wonder it was called the Skyland City.

Yellow light cast flaming shadows out of the infinite reckoning of windows. I craned my head to the side but in no way could I confirm where the city had its outskirts on the other side. It stretched into the vast distance of a new wondrous lifestyle.

I had craned so low to my side, I almost fell off the horse, and saw Blake's smirk out of the corner of my eye.

"You're going to swallow all the flies and not leave any for the sparrows, if you don't close your mouth soon."

I clenched my jaw shut instantly and sat back up straight. How could I have let him see how stunned I was? A princess's composure was important to instil confidence and indisputable bargaining powers.

The city's magnitude compelled me unintentionally to stare at it again though. Faint howls seemed to creep outside the gates like hungry spirits who weren't allowed inside. Never mind guards, handcuffs or fangs keeping me imprisoned, if I got lost in that maze of a city, I might never find my way out of the area, as buildings rose up looking like a hedgehog's back. As the horse swayed me closer to the city, I also couldn't distinguish any particular roads or streets. It seemed as if the inhabitants had thrown a stone at random and where it landed, they had built their home. The smell in the air was that of iron and maybe even a hint of blood and the ominous all-enveloping darkness, made the hairs on my arms stand up.

The large double oak gates swung open as we neared the curtain wall surrounding the city. The guards bowed deeply until we had passed them before quickly closing the gates behind us. As we clip-clopped over the cobblestones further into the city, the howls died down, window shutters closed and lights dissipated for as far ahead as the sound of the hooves could be heard.

"It's as if they'd never seen a Fae before," I snorted.

Blake chuckled loudly. "I don't think that's why they are afraid. Father has a bit of a merciless reputation." He scratched his forehead nervously, glancing around him. "We shouldn't make them go into hiding for long; a new day will begin soon. Haya!" He kicked the horse and jerked in the saddle, making it break into a canter.

Eventually, after we had turned what seemed like an endless number of corners, a grand building, ten times bigger than the others, appeared in view. The steel gates surrounding it opened for Blake and he rode inside, jumping down and handing the reins to one of the guards.

"This way," he said, gesturing with his hand for me to be escorted into his palace.

I turned my nose the other way and sighed before I reluctantly felt agreeable to dismount.

"Quickly now," he urged, as if the Alpha was awaiting our visit.

He rushed me inside, through winding corridors with portraits of wolves and human Alphas hanging on the walls and finally halted in front of two tall double doors which loomed up in front of us, covered with engraved and extremely detailed images of wolves hunting animals in the forest. The two guards in front of them hesitated to move when they saw me, but parted and left the way clear at a nod from Blake.

Blake almost launched himself at the doors and burst into the room as they parted. The massive hall in front of us featured three thrones on a raised platform at the far end. On the largest middle throne sat a sturdy man – it was Alpha Moon.

He swiftly got off his seat when we arrived and took a few steps towards us, but stopped abruptly. His torso twitched and he fell onto his knees. Fur started to spurt out of his clothes and when he looked up at us, fangs burst through his gums.

"Okay," Blake pronounced, hurriedly turning me around and pushing me out of the room. "We'll have to come back tomorrow."

He closed the doors almost in panic, keeping his hands on the door handles to ensure the doors stayed shut.

"Don't let him out!" he shouted at the guards who hastily slid their spears into the looped handles to block anyone exiting.

What the heck was going on?

CHAPTER 14

I f I wasn't mistaken, the look on his face was almost
that of embarrassment. He pulled his fingers
through his wavy brown hair.

"Um, alright…the Moon Guestroom is over
here."

"The Moon Guestroom?"

He tapped irritably with his foot. "Yes why?
Would you prefer the Sun Guestroom?"

I was taken aback. I had thought I was going to
be kept in a dungeon similar to Master Crowland's
establishment, but a Guestroom sounded great. "Yes,
in fact I would. I like the sound of Sun better than
Moon."

"Fine." He took long strides down the corridor
making me rush to keep up with him.

I could hear his bare feet stomp onto the red
carpet that dressed the halls and as I looked down at

them, I saw fur starting to coat their surface. My eyes almost popped out of their sockets as I witnessed the Alpha heir slowly shifting.

Why was he in such a rush?

Next, he flailed a hairy paw at one of the guards standing at the bottom of some stairs leading high up to another floor.

"You there, take her to the Sun Guestroom. Remain on guard duty outside our guest's room tonight and don't let anyone in."

In? What about out!

He bowed in a rapid motion and I could see more fur curling out of his skin around his collar. "I have some urgent matters to attend to and I'll come for you tomorrow, late evening."

He ran off as if there was a fire up his arse.

When he was out of sight, my mind immediately started to plan an escape. I looked around, but saw the blue caped guard approaching swiftly. He was in his prime with a dense muscular build, so I could forget sprinting past him. Ushered into the guestroom by his firm hand pushing at my back, I almost stumbled onto the beige wooden floor. No questions were asked about my comfort before he slammed the iron door shut and I heard the ring handle on the other side of the door squeak as it swung, bashing iron against iron.

I spun round as I walked further into the room and my eyes popped wide open – Yellow!

Curtains, walls, bedding, nightstands, rugs, chest of drawers…everything was painted like the hottest day of summer. It felt sinister, yet somehow serene. Blake must love the sun, although he also had a Moon Guestroom. I wondered how that was decorated; like the night with a bright dotted sky so his guest could howl at the moon without having to go outside?

I skipped round the bed and towards the four-paned window to assess my surroundings, and how long it might take me to break free.

I was one floor up with a manageable jump to the grass below, the gardens had a few trees scattered all the way to the fence where I could hide, and a fence could be climbed if I took extra care over the spiked top. "Not impossible if I wasn't seen by any guards and…" I looked the other way, "nope," I couldn't see anyone around. I was still wearing black and the morning was still dark, so I only needed to stay in the shadows, blending in with the tree trunks.

I tugged at the metal latch of the bottom frame, jerking the window upwards. It didn't budge. I bent my knees to get greater leverage in an effort to force it open, but it just didn't yield an opening wider than one where I could just stick my fingers out. A waft of a mouldy smell coming from the grooves clung to my nose. This window hadn't been opened for a long time, or perhaps ever. At this rate, I would be struggling with it until tomorrow night before I could press myself through any sort of gap.

Okay, next plan.

I turned around and looked at what items there were in the room. A lamp base crafted out of polished stone on the nightstand looked hefty. I removed the glass covering the oil-soaked wick before picking it up. All my muscle power had to go into the lift and it was going to be a challenge swinging it out of the window. I poured the oil from the copper container into the plant in the corner of the room and darted back to the window again, but hesitated just before hitting the glass. It was going to be noisy. I raced back to the nightstand, dropping the lamp onto the bed whilst I took off the pillowcase before wrapping it around the stone lamp base. It wasn't going to make much of a difference, but it could dampen the noise of the smashing somewhat.

Like a sledgehammer, I swung the heavy monstrosity at the window. The wooden panel dividing the panes broke on the window's right-hand side along with the two panes. It wasn't big enough for me to fit through, so I hammered out some more of the sharp glass edges to clear my exit and with a giant step, I heaved myself up to stand on the windowsill and snake my way outside. Another short jump and I was free of the dog's den.

I didn't hang around and darted for the trees, pressing myself up against the bark. I looked around, but I couldn't see anyone.

So far so good.

I made it to the fence, launching myself as high as I could off the ground, gripping a tight fistful of the iron bars to hoist myself upwards.

Suddenly, I felt something pinching around my foot, preventing me from pulling it upwards. My foot was stuck. I looked down and saw two deep green eyes staring up at me while the wolf's teeth were clamped around my boot.

How did he get here so blinking fast?

I hadn't heard him nearing me at all. There was no mistaking who the grey wolf with the white patches of fur was; I could recognise Blake in his wolf form by now. When I didn't move, he growled lightly at me, not threateningly, but to say I needed to step down from the fence, or he wouldn't let go of my foot.

Not a prisoner, yeah right!

I wiggled my foot, prompting him to let go of it before I could step down. I had already established with certainty that I couldn't outrun a wolf, but I was bloody well going to try.

I made a sudden run for it, sprinting for the gate but a whole pack of wolves appeared from all sides, closing me in. My heart pumped fast. I had nowhere to go.

The wolves didn't look menacing nor did they show any teeth. They just stood there watching me after what seemed to have been an unexpected shift to come to their Alpha heir's aid. Fabric from half torn clothes still flapped from some of their waists, some had their capes twisted onto their fronts and others even had their belts still on with their swords dragging over the grass when they moved.

Blake broke away from the circle of wolves slowly to sneak his way closer to me. Without any sudden movement he grasped his jaw gently around my wrist, his teeth only tickling my veins. I followed him as he led me towards the palace.

"Damn dog," I muttered, feeling his slobber smudging my skin. "You got me; you can shift into a human now."

He halted in his stride for a moment but then continued leading me inside in his wolf form. He obviously didn't trust me not to run, which was wise, because as soon as he let me out of his sight, I planned to try escaping again.

At the door, his human guards took over the escort service and Blake loped off into the Skyland City's morning glare. I covered my eyes against the sun, but couldn't see where he went. Nor was it important to know since I obviously wasn't going to be deciding where I was heading next. The four blue capes stomped behind me with clanking armours as they led me through corridors with vaulted ceilings and past portrait covered walls stretching out between hundreds of doorframes.

This is just madness. I must get out of the wolf territory.

Two wide doors stood fully open at the end of the last hallway we walked down, their dark wood reminding me of the cork bungs used for the rarest wine bottles presented on special occasions held in the Fairola palace. That instantly made my mouth dry. Wine would be nice right now…even though it was super early in the morning.

But as my father used to say; wine is always appropriate in bad moments – and this definitely qualified as one.

I was pushed into the room, past the enormous doors, but the guards didn't enter. They turned their backs on me and stood outside.

In the middle of the hall before me, was a long table. It was decorated for a breakfast feast with a tall vase of flowers in the centre, two five-armed candelabras on either side and silver trays laden with food all set on a white table cloth that was ironed to perfection.

This is the princess treatment I'm talking about.

Rather worryingly though, was the other person sitting at the table. He had a Skully pack tattoo of a howling wolf on his enormous biceps, but wasn't a warrior wearing a green cape. Why was he here?

His whole demeanour was playfully mischievous. Dark brown eyes stared at me like a teasing older brother's even though I had never seen him before. He clenched a pipe between his thumb and finger, lifting it to his mouth to inhale a deep breath, and I noticed he had a wide leather bracelet with studs on his wrist. He brought the pipe out of his mouth and adjusted the woolly hat that he for some reason he was wearing indoors in summer, and only half way down his ears. From one of them a ring hooped through his earlobe. His brown hair was sticking out, curling over his collar and looked greasy. Unshaven, tattooed, he had holes in his leather trousers and a top without sleeves that wasn't tucked in – who was this disgrace?

"Early bird too, Princess?"

He knew me.

I brushed some leaves off that had stuck to my sleeve. "No, not really."

He hid a huge smile by inhaling and puffing out more smoke. "Trying to escape so soon?"

So he knew I was a captive.

He laid his pipe down on his plate. "I at least waited two days before trying to escape myself. Spoiler alert! There's no way out."

CHAPTER 15

I frowned.

He was a prisoner too?

I folded my arms across my body, inspecting him in silence. The wolf shifter had plonked his arse down on the Alpha's chair. It was a robust wooden throne with its back carved out like an enraged wolf showing teeth - the Skyland emblem.

To occupy that seat was a brave...or a stupid gesture.

He cleared his throat. "Are you just going to stand there? Come and sit." He waved his hand out to gesture at all the dishes lined up on the table.

I took slow and careful steps towards the stranger.

He looked me up and down as he chuckled. "I don't bite, Princess. Not in my human form, anyway."

"Who are you?"

"Ouch, I feel offended. Not only have we played together, but I thought my reputation would have preceded me."

I narrowed my eyes to look deeper at him. "Scratch?"

"In the flesh."

This was Skully's oldest son, his heir. Imprisoned by the Skyland wolf pack.

This can't be good.

I had played a lot with him many years ago when Father, on several occasions, had invited the Alphas to council meetings. Blake had been all work but Scratch and I had played hide and seek around the palace and being a wolf, he had cheated of course. He had been charming then, but look at him now! Although, I guess his smile and glittering brown eyes were still as charming as ever.

"Now, will you sit down and join me for breakfast?"

I snapped out of my reminiscences. I didn't know whether to laugh or cry, I was so relieved that he was here. I ran around the table, and he stood up holding out his arms when I came at him, throwing myself into his embrace. I burrowed my face in the crook of his shoulder, his warm arms envelop all of me, and his cheek nestled on my head.

"There, there, we'll get out of this…somehow."

I pulled away from his chest. "There's no point."

"Well, I never! From you, Pudding?"

That made me break out in laughter, with which he joined in. He knew me to be very stubborn, and Pudding was a nickname he had used for me back when we were kids because of the number of treats I'd convinced him to steal for me from Clarence. I had always been a bottomless pit when it came to dessert.

"Scratch, why are they holding you here? Why the attack on the Fae? What is the Skyland pack up to?"

He sighed deeply. "Let's sit down. You must be starving." He leaned over the table to grab a glass and poured me some wine which definitely made him meet with my full approval. He also pushed a plate piled with sunflower seed bread towards me. "So how have you been, Pudding?"

"What? No! I don't want to be wined and dined; I want to know what is going on."

"Sorry, just wanted to find out how much you knew already. You know…to ease you in on the bad news."

"You mean about my father?"

"Okay, so you know about that."

"Know about it? I saw it with my own eyes!"

"Aww Pudding, I'm so sorry."

His puppy dog eyes looked sincere. It riled me.

"Sorry? If your pack had not attacked the Skyland pack, maybe nothing of this would have happened."

His eyes turned a shade darker and his face got all serious. "We attack? No, they…"

Four blue caped guards lead by a commanding officer suddenly rushed inside. The guard who had led me here and then had stood guard was catching up behind them, shouting that he hadn't known Scratch was in here. The Commander, showing his status with a white circle tag on his uniform representing a full moon, looked panicked. The look on his face frightened me. What did it mean?

They all forced themselves on Scratch, holding him down. I curled my back further into my seat, hoping they would leave me alone, but it seemed that they only came for him. Scratch wasn't subdued by their attempts at restraint though when the five men jumped him, but fought back, managing to fell two of the men with knockout blows to their faces. He had height in his favour, being at least half a head taller than the others. He fought ferociously as the guards came at him from every angle. He looked strong with bulging muscles, as he withstood the guards' punches. He held them off for longer than I thought he would, but then he started to tire.

With only the commander left standing, he engaged in a one-on-one battle, blocking and punching every other go. The Commander stuck a compact fist into Scratch's stomach, making him fold double, but he didn't buckle to the floor. Pausing a second to suck air into his lungs, he countered, returning the attack in a mad frenzy.

"Leave me alone!" he roared, kicking round, hitting the Commander square in the back.

The Commander flew to the floor, but as he got up, so did the others in unison. They all attacked at the same time, holding Scratch down onto both his knees with two of the men pulling his arms back, pinning his chest out and pressing a foot each against his back. The Commander; an older man with sparse grey hair and wrinkles, yet seemingly adept at his job, approached Scratch slowly, wiping blood from his lip. He crouched down to keep his face near Scratch's face and angrily pulled the beige woolly hat off, letting the greasy neck-long hair spring in every direction.

The Commander grabbed a fist full and tugged it

back. "And I had thought that we were starting to get along."

Scratch spat in his face.

The Commander looked repulsed, wiping the spit off. "Take him away!"

The guards clamped cuffs around his wrists, wrestling him to try and get him to move.

"Athroxane!" Scratch shouted, "Remember that you are a Fae princess and…"

The Commander swiftly snatched up one of the silver candelabras, bringing it down hard on Scratch's head. Scratch's shouting stopped abruptly and his body sagged to the floor.

The Commander had silenced him on purpose. There was something he hadn't wanted Scratch to tell me.

But what?

I knew I was a Fae princess; that wasn't a secret. I felt ashamed for not having helped Scratch fight off the guards, but I had thought that the two of us had no chance against the five of them. After I had seen how strong he was and how good he was at fighting, I wondered whether I had missed my chance to escape. Now they were dragging him away by the arms across the floor, leaving me alone in a big after-battle void with my adrenaline still pumping and my heart throbbing.

After the trauma had settled, I thought I had lost my appetite, but I was starving. The thought of Scratch's safety and what they were doing to him was at the back of my mind as I ravenously ripped at the bread, stuffing my mouth and washing it down with wine. I threw myself equally into the cheese and fruits, which had been beautifully displayed on large platters. When I was sated, I sank back down onto the chair, my horrible situation nagging on my mind once more. The food had started to take hold in my stomach though and my energies were flowing back.

Right. I need another escape plan.

I had been impatient. Scratch had waited for two days before he had attempted to prison-break this sky-high city. He had probably been wise enough to first observe his surroundings and assess his opportunities whereas I had been rash. But I also really didn't want to be here, and on top of it, I had the time pressure of returning to Master Crowland. I still had the Fae Mother scroll around my thigh so if I could find Master Crowland before he found me and pass it over, just maybe, I had a chance of keeping all my body parts where they were supposed to be.

If I couldn't sneak out alone, utilising my strength and agility, I would need help. Scratch's help. Instead of desperately spending my hours looking for a way out, I was going to search for a way in. They were most likely keeping him in another guestroom or in the dungeons. Finding him would yield the best odds of getting out.

I stood up determinedly, resolute not to become a victim of a wolf pack. The day I died, I was going to die on the battlefield, fighting for my people, not from withering away trapped inside a wolf palace. My heels clicked on the marble floor as I walked towards the guards at the door. I was eager to make anything happen, which could bring me closer to freedom.

I crossed my arms irately, staring at the guards. "Now what?"

They looked at each other questioningly, until one of them spoke. "You're free to go anywhere you want, except outside the palace walls, Your Majesty."

"Fine. Then I want to see Scratch."

"Or to his room," the other guard added.

Perfect! Stupid buffoon, letting me know that Scratch did have a room inside the palace and was not in any dungeon.

"Fine. Anywhere else I'm not allowed?"

"Well, I'm sure the Alpha's wing is off limits too."

"What about a garden? Does the palace feature any green spaces?"

"Yes."

"Well, take me there then!"

On the way, I scrutinised every corridor we walked along, eyeing every object and trying my best to look into rooms with open doors.

There must be a clue somewhere.

I found a tranquil area in the garden and sat down on a bench, the guards constantly watching me from a short distance away. I sat there for a long while, watching the palace grounds, smelling the flowers and listening to the birds' morning song as it turned into the noon lunchtime chirp. In all the time I was there, I didn't see anything that would benefit me in an escape bid. The place was well fortified and there were blue capes everywhere, patrolling the premises at intervals.

I sighed, knowing how hopeless it all was. If I only knew what they wanted from me; although, could it be anything other than gaining a leverage for power? If they only knew that I was no longer a great bargaining tool. The Fae wanted me dead and probably welcomed the suggestion that the wolves execute me, which would spare them the time. The council had always wanted more power and with Father and I out of their way, nothing could stop them from dominating Fairola Kingdom.

For lunch and dinner I was taken back to the dining hall and presented with the same royal feast as I had had for breakfast; but I had to have it alone.

All the time I was wondering where Blake was and why he hadn't visited me to tell me what was going on. What other important matters were there that he had to let the princess of Fae wait? I missed having people around me. I missed my Father and our friends; I longed for the servants, for Merry Kerri and almost even Clarence. But Father was dead, my bodyguard Vargo was dead and I could only hope that Andreas hadn't died a horrible death too.

When darkness settled outside as night approached, I couldn't bear it anymore. I put down my book that I had borrowed from the library, and from where I lay in the bed, I looked out of the window that had been repaired from this morning.

I must attempt to flee. I can't give up.

I had to keep attempting to escape every night for the rest of my life if need be. I was never going to stop fighting, never give up.

I strode towards the windowsill and looked up at the stars in the clear night sky. I tapped my fingers on the wooden frame as I pondered.

So, all the wolves were on high alert because of me being a flight risk, meaning that if I were to walk outside with two guards at my back, the rest of the wolves wouldn't bother me too much? That meant I only had to kill two wolf shifters and then try to find my way out rather than face the entire pack.

I decided that it was one way of attempting to

break out even if I knew it wasn't a great one. I pulled the door open and rushed past the two guards that were standing outside my door. They raced after me, but kept a royal distance.

"It's a lovely night. I want to gaze at the stars for a while."

"Of course, Your Majesty," one of them answered as they tagged along.

I made sure I walked calmly for long enough so that other guards could register my chaperones. Then, turning a corner, I sprinted with as much speed as I could muster towards the front gates.

Having expected the threat to be behind me, I failed to detect what I had in front of me and slammed straight into something hard that hadn't been there moments earlier. My sight blackened and blurred but I managed to stay conscious. In the haze of greys I was aware of two butch arms sporting the black full moon emblem on their shoulders, circling under my armpits and dragging me across the courtyard.

Black Moon guards, these were the Alpha's security detail, and not to be messed with. Dragged over grass, marble flooring, red carpets and then black marble, I was finally dumped down like a filthy beggar onto the floor.

It was cold and the room was dark. Dizzy and disorientated with my head hurting, I pressed my hands against the floor to heave my chest up. In my swaying vision, clouded with yellow dots, I could see the three steps up to a throne. I looked higher upwards and saw Alpha Clifford Moon sitting on his throne, his face that of a wolf seeing red.

CHAPTER 16

The Alpha's intense eyes demanded submission
worthy of his status; a potent force holding me
down on my knees.

"You aren't going anywhere until you've made
me a blood curse cord."

Bloody hell, he was seeing red.

I twitched my head to the side, staring daggers at
Blake who was standing at his father's side.

To ask a favour? My sweet royal ass!

He avoided me, looking down at his hands that
were clasped level with his crotch.

Anger was boiling in my gut when I turned back
to Alpha Moon. "The council has forbidden all Fae
from using blood curse cords. Only the King can
overrule our laws."

"The King is dead. You're their queen now.
Overrule it!"

Well, there was one problem with that; I was no longer hailed as queen by my people and giving the Alpha a red cord, certainly wasn't going to grace me with any forgiveness.

I had to be strong. I stared back at him with the same intensity. "No!"

He stood up from his throne, looking like he wanted to punch something...or someone. His chin was taut and all his muscles tense. He moved closer to me as he deliberated, slowly descending the steps of the platform.

"I'll write a parchment to the council, to Courtess Flamirna stating I'm keeping you prisoner. With some insignificant trade, I can ensure that you'll get back to your castle with your honour intact. No one will know you fled from the battlefield."

A tremor ran through me; a complete exoneration was at my fingertips. The only one who could screw it up for me was Master Crowland, if we ever crossed paths in the future and he recognised me.

But Alpha Moon didn't know that.

If he had, he wouldn't have given me this offer, knowing he could get caught out. An Alpha who is lying to his pack would rouse many challengers to his throne; and that would surely cost him more than a blood curse cord.

Now the tables had turned, I desperately wanted to help him and I would go to any lengths to get home, but how to get around my shortcomings? I didn't know how to make a blood curse cord.

"I'll accept your offer, but I'll need to find another Fae to make a cord for your curse. A queen can't…"

"No! It must be you!"

I startled back from his outburst.

This one's crazy.

His demand would force me to have to confess my ineptness, unless I refused to cooperate. What else could I do?

Refusing though, might only get me held up here for longer – maybe for life, however long that might be after a refusal.

One thing was sure though, I wasn't going to agree to any terms whilst still on my knees; that's where I drew a line of disgrace. I brought up my first knee, and the Alpha signalled to the alerted guard to allow it. I stood up straight, and pushed some tousled hair back with a sassy flick of my hand.

I cleared my throat regally. "I would need some training."

The Alpha gave me all his attention now. "What do you need?"

"To learn how to make a red spell cord." I scratched the back of my neck nervously, awaiting his reaction.

He just stood there, looking at me, breathing slowly.

I wish he would say something.

It was like a spell had frozen everyone; not even his eyes moved inside their sockets.

He backed up so that he could slump down onto his throne. He bit on his thumbnail and looked utterly lost. "You don't know how to break the curse," he muttered.

I folded my arms over my chest. "Curse? What curse?"

"The Fae King placed a curse on my blood. You

must reverse it!" He kept whipping his finger in the air towards me, and now I understood why he was so angry.

"I can't break a blood curse my father made. It's too strong."

He flew to his feet once more, twisting erratically in his anger. "You can!"

My fear dissipated. He was just making me bloody annoyed now for wasting my time. "Well, yeah, it's possible, but that takes spells and power and a medallion and…"

"You will do it!" His voice bounced between the stone walls, echoing a few times before it settled.

I believe that even the flames from the scattered braziers in the room shied away in terror.

I turned away from him abruptly; my nose in the air. "No!" Then turned to stare at him. "That's not what I signed up for."

"Let me remind you that you didn't sign up to be here in the first place. None of this is voluntary. You'll do as I command."

"Since when does a filthy dog tell a Fae Queen what to do?"

"Since right now. Guards!" he shouted, although they were standing close to my back already. "Take the Fae Queen to her guestroom, and don't let her out until she has given you her solemn word that she'll break the curse."

Yep. Refusing got me locked up.

The guards grabbed my arms and started to drag me backwards.

"Wait!" I yelled. I started to sweat and my forehead became clammy with panic as I fought to pull my arms free. "I challenge you to an Alpha

Duel!"

It sent gasps around the hall like a ghostly hollow.

Oh my god, what had I done?

CHAPTER 17

Alpha Moon looked me up and down as a cunning smile spread across his face. I wondered what he made of my small frame and soft curves. My heart pounded hard as I waited for his response.

"I accept your challenge with a condition; if you win, you're free to leave and you'll rule over my pack but if I win, you'll make me the cord."

The Alpha relished at his victory. He had me right where he wanted.

Demon Dogs!

Shock prevented me from replying before he bellowed orders once again. "Take her to her room and prepare her for the duel. We'll fight tomorrow night!"

The horror weakened my senses and made me totally mindless. I couldn't even remember the guards dragging me back to my Sun guestroom; whether I had walked on my own two feet or been carried, I couldn't say.

I slumped down onto the yellow bedspread, staring at nothing.

I have just dug myself down a deeper hole.

Now Alpha Moon only needed to cover it with soil to bury me alive.

The rumour of the Skyland Alpha and the Fae Queen duelling was going to spread like wildfire across all the kingdoms and Crowland's crew was going to be on my back faster than the sun burns my fair skin during high season.

I swallowed down a dry lump in my throat.

I'm dead.

I cleared my throat; dread coated my tongue with a bitter taste.

I can't breathe.

I was tired. It was late, or early morning – I didn't know that either.

Suddenly, Blake barged in through the door and shut it hard behind him. His metal medallion that he always wore swung against his bare torso. I didn't care that he looked annoyed at me; I threw myself into his arms.

More stupidity!

Why had I launched myself into the embrace of my capturer? Had I momentarily forgotten that he was the Alpha's son?

Why did I feel so relieved to see him?

I shook some sense into my heavy head and pulled away before he could push me off. "You have a strange heartbeat." I tried my best to sound casual.

"Yes, wolf shifters have two hearts. You should know that. You should also know that we're stronger than Fae, faster than horses and men like my father have been trained to kill since they were young boys."

There was no trace of his light-hearted charming mien as I looked at his face. A nervous twine knotted in my stomach like a slithering snake unsure as to whether it was being attacked or not.

Why had he come to my room?

He circled around me, walking towards the darkness outside the window, frantically pulling his fingers through his hair. "What the hell have you done?"

"I was dead anyway," I barked in my defence. "I don't know how to make a red cord!"

"We could have solved it together! But challenging the Alpha…" He shook his head wildly. "Not even I can get you out of that death."

"He can't kill me. He needs me for the cord, remember."

"Well, he can get bloody close!" He almost spat in my face.

"Hey, cool it."

He started pacing the room. "Normally, I would fight a duel on behalf of a woman, but against my father, I can't!"

"Because if you win, I'll be free, but you can't free me as you too need me to break the curse, don't you? It's a blood curse, you must also be affected by it."

That reminded me that my father had placed the curse on them during the last moment of his life, and I didn't even know why. I had only seen that my father had fought the Alpha, but it hadn't seemed vicious. They had been friends for many years. Why had they swung a sword at one another?

"Yes, I also have it," he said, irritably. "But that's not the reason as to why I'd prefer it if you weren't beaten to death."

I bit my lip, wanting desperately to ask my burning question. "So what does the curse do, anyway?"

Blake turned round, pacing across the room to lower himself onto the bed.

He sighed gloomily. "It hinders me from howling at the moon and from sunbathing at noon."

"What? That doesn't sound so bad."

"Roxie, I'm cursed to be a human at night and a wolf by day. That's why I prefer the Moon guestroom; the times when I'm in my human form. I'm never fully in control over what I do when I'm a wolf." He smiled a little with a look of reminiscence. "But father finds it harder to control himself than I do. So, I lock him in somewhere most days."

"Doesn't he get mad?"

"Raging."

We both smiled at the same time.

I should have been thinking about the duel, but thoughts about why Blake had called me Roxie were going through my mind instead. Only a few select close friends ever called me that. I thought about Andreas and Kerri, wondering how they were faring.

It felt as if all my defences were breaking. It was hard to be distant with Blake when he was so comforting.

I yawned, as I too, lowered myself onto the bed. "You do know who has the grimoire that tells of how to break a blood curse?"

"What? You know? No, who?"

"Courtess Flamirna. She won't give it to anyone

else though, not even me, and I can't steal the tome from the Courtess of the Fae Council."

Blake pulled something out of his leg pocket. "Like you could with this one, for example."

He held out the golden cylinder with the scroll, which was said to have been written by the Fae Mother herself; the one I had removed from the North Temple. I had completely forgotten about that. He must have taken it from me when I had been asleep.

I stared at it as he held it up. "What will you do with it? We have to put it back."

"I think I'll hold onto it for now; for safekeeping, just in case you decide to attempt another one of your escapes."

That dampened my chilled mood. He was smiling as if this situation was funny. He was a bastard after all, manipulating me with his good looks and his protecting demeanour, but when it came to it, he didn't hand me any favours. He was just a rock in my shoe.

Curse him. Curse all wolves!

Tomorrow night, I'll kill the Alpha, and make them all kneel and kiss my feet.

"Get out! I need to sleep." I pointed a firm finger at the door.

He suddenly became rueful and made an acknowledging blink at me before standing up and shuffling his feet towards the door. He opened it but stopped in the doorway and twisted his head round. "I'll come by with your kit tomorrow after supper. I guess you'll want a sword and knives and a new black combat suit?"

If I had answered him, my tears would have

started to fall. I could barely hold it together as it was, so I just nodded, keeping my gaze at the floor.

He walked out and closed the door gently. Muffled by it, I heard him instruct the guards not to let anyone in or out until lunchtime tomorrow.

Tears from each eye had escaped and were falling down on my cheeks. I dried them off quickly with the palm of my hand. I dived under the bedcovers and wrapped my arms around my knees.

Today was going to end with me having eaten and slept like a queen, but tomorrow I was going to be beaten up like a worthless servant.

CHAPTER 18

Jeez! Someone's really going for it, knocking on my door. Even though the sun blasted right through my window, amplified by the yellow décor, I was still startled into wakefulness. As my awareness of what today might bring came rushing to my head, a sense of gloomy anxiety enveloped my inner peace. However, the thought of my inevitable death was pushed to the back of my mind a little by the heavenly smell of fresh bread.

"Yes! Come in!" If the knocking became any more fervent, I would develop a permanent headache – not what I needed today.

A gentleman in tight white trousers tucked into high black boots, and wearing a light-blue tailcoat entered the room. He was balancing the largest silver tray I'd ever seen on one upheld hand.

"Good day, Fae Queen," the man greeted.

The servant had black hair sleeked back from a centre parting, and a funny-looking straight-combed moustache.

Good day? I looked out of the window. Yes, the sun was high in the sky. "Did I miss breakfast?"

The servant put the tray down on a sturdy round oak table standing by the side of the window. "Master Moon…Junior…" he said, turning to stand stiffly by the side of my bed with his hands folded behind his back. "I was told that you were still resting and weren't to be disturbed." He remained silently by my bedside to the point where it was awkward. "Will that be all, Fae Queen?"

"Yes, yes, of course, you are dismissed."

Where were my manners, I had probably left them in the gutter when sleeping rough, or in Crowland's dungeon cell. At least the servant had done one good thing for me – he had reminded me that I was the Fae Queen, and damn it, I was going to fight like one tonight.

He had also brought me a gorgeous lunch of course and it smelt divine. I jumped out of bed, rushing to see what they had provided for me. The first thing I took notice of was a single red rose laid on a serviette on top of an empty white plate.

Odd, why the rose?

I thought back to last night when Blake had reprimanded me for not knowing enough about wolves. Maybe the rose symbolised something to them. To a Fae it was given as an endearment to show affection, but I didn't expect that from Blake.

My stomach made a sound I'd never heard it do before, so I tore into the bread, dipping it in the butter and letting the flavours melt together on my tongue. I shoved a slice of cheese into my mouth between the bites of bread. It was soft and semi-cured. There were grapes and a glass of freshly pressed orange juice and when I lifted the silver cloche, I found a plate of beans, a grilled tomato, two sausages and three slices of bacon.

Well, if you think that I should know more about wolf shifters, you should know that Fae are vegetarians.

The humour of the mocking voice in my mind made me feel a bit lighter in spirit. Yet, I did steal a second glance at the meat, licking my lips. Maybe I should eat it; I had heard it gave you energy, and the Fae Mother knew I needed it for this evening.

I sighed. That the thought had even crossed my mind was a disgrace. Who was I? I could never eat the flesh of other innocent animals. No! Barbaric! I wasn't going to allow this experience to change who I was. I put the rose aside and took the fork out of its serviette wrapping and pierced it into the tomato, moving it onto the plate from which I had cleared the rose. I tilted the plate with the meat so that only the beans slid across to the other plate too, leaving a distinct line of tomato sauce to ensure the beans stayed clear of any meat juices. The cloche went back on after that, so that the dead animals who had suffered to feed the wolves wouldn't be staring at me.

I was still chewing on my last mouthful when the frantic knocks hit on the door again.

That stuck up servant hadn't heard of – knock and wait.

"Yes, for all that is holy, come in!"

And my father always said I was impatient.

The servant scurried in like he had before, as if he was on a busy schedule, or as if he thought he would turn into a frog if he was in my presence too long. He dropped off a sword and a shield by leaning them against the wall next to the doorframe before making his way to the tray, clearing the empty dishes and hoisting the tray into the air. As if he was surfing on a smooth wave, he flowed out of the room, leaving me to deal with this terrifying reality alone. I remained sitting on the chair, my eyes transfixed on the weapons he'd left behind. They were for me: to fight and kill.

The sword hilt was made of silver and had a pommel shaped like a howling wolf's head. The sheath was wide, its entire surface daintily crafted with gorgeous swirling patterns where some of the junctures were adorned with sapphires or mountain crystals. The shield next to it matched it in style and would easily cover three of me behind its circumference.

My hands started to tremble as they lay on my knees. This made the reality of the duel so very physical. They had provided me with weapons and had started to prep me for combat with the Alpha. No one was bluffing.

CHAPTER 19

I stood immobile, suffering with every beat of my heart, staring at the steel weapons. They were shiny; I would even guess that they were newly crafted. Blake had made sure I was provided with the best, and not just some leftover rusty blade forged centuries ago. I finally comprehended how seriously the wolves honoured the duel. This was real; it was going to happen. I was going to use that sword and shield in real combat, in a fight to the death against the Skyland Alpha. I felt sick to my stomach. I couldn't even imagine how this could end well.

Was I really going to die tonight?

Maybe that was better than having body parts cut off one by one, as punishment by Master Crowland. At least I wasn't going to die being his slave.

I swallowed down my fear - or at least I tried to and approached the weapons as if they were about to combust into flames. I enveloped the hilt with my dainty fingers and held onto the sheath as I pulled the blade out.

Gosh, it's heavy.

I swung some test cuts through the air. With adrenaline pumping, maybe I could manage a few blows, but I had always preferred a bow or at least a long bladed dagger. I supposed it was considered cheating if I made a blue cord to wrap around the tip. After a few more swings, testing the sword's balance, I glanced at the shield.

I had never used a shield any of the times I had sparred with my father. He used to say it was for strong men. Women use poison, bows or backstabbing, but in case I did get caught in a fight, he'd thought I should at least know how to use a dagger; so we sparred with a dagger or without any weapons.

I tilted the shield off the wall so I could reach the handle strap, but as I shoved my arm through the first strap, fisting my hand around the second, to try and lift it up, I discovered it was too heavy to hold with one arm.

Why had Blake provided me with this monstrosity? He must have known I wasn't strong enough to handle it.

Perhaps that was his message - not to use it. He knew his father's strengths and weaknesses and my speed of attack would give me the advantage I needed, instead of being on the defensive, hiding behind a shield. But that theory was all well and good if I trusted him. It could also just be that he wanted me to fail, making sure that I had no opportunity to defend myself. I got worked up once more, my breathing speeding up and my nerves making me shake.

I must die a death worthy of a Fae Queen.

I grabbed the hilt with both my hands and moved around the room, alternating in kicking the air and stabbing at it. The sword needed to become my best friend before the evening came.

I spent the afternoon sparring and resting, sparring and resting. The angrier I got the more I lashed out at things in the room, carving large chunks out of the chest of drawers, scarring the wall and completely killing the pillows. I still didn't feel ready when it was getting late and a wolf was let into my room.

"Oh, it's you. Hello Blake."

Soundlessly, he strolled around the room, seeming to inspect all the damage I had inflicted upon the furniture. He approached the bed and stood on his hind legs with his front paws on the mattress, glancing at the duvet feathers; a sight where it seemed a hundred ducks had been plucked. He jumped off and circled the carpet before lying down with his jaw on his front paws.

"Nice doggy."

I relaxed somewhat, relieved he seemed to be in control of himself even after his inspection. He was watching me so I smiled at him, feeling awkward being observed by him in wolf form without being able to communicate. After a while of not knowing what to do, and the wolf not moving, I crossed the room to look out of the window. I hadn't looked out over the green display of multiple shades of pine trees and silver birch for very long when a sharp bark resounded behind me. I turned around to check whether Blake was still in control of himself. He had lifted his head up and his green eyes were staring at me. He twisted towards the sword that I had leaned back against the wall and barked again.

"What? Do you want me to thank you for those? You were the one getting me in to this mess in the first place. It's your fault I even have to fight."

Unexpectedly, he winced a bit. Looking into his eyes, somehow I got the feeling he didn't like this situation any more than I did. I moaned out my frustration and turned back to stare out of the window again until I heard another scraping noise. I flung an angry glower his way but he didn't notice as he was too busy scratching at the sheath to make the sword fall over before grabbing the leather clad hilt in his mouth and dragging it my way.

"You've come to spy on my battle technique?"

He deliberately dropped the hilt on my foot and it struck painfully at my ankle bone. His bark this time was longer and more pleading.

"Isn't the state of the room proof enough?"

He didn't look, but instead growled at me, baring his teeth.

Maybe I shouldn't have pointed that out.

He sat down, his tail tucked close to his body - not wagging. He wasn't impressed. The way he sat observing me, it kind of looked like he was waiting for me to stop being silly and to show him what I had.

The sword was still lying on my foot so I flicked it up and caught it in my hand. I saw his tail twitch just then. Had he tried to hide a happy wag?

I slammed the sword tip down, digging it into the thick woolly carpet, balanced my hands on either side of the hilt and cartwheeled over the sword. Immediately, I kneeled down to follow the momentum, yanking the sword out and slashing it through the air.

I stopped abruptly, letting the heavy sword fall to the floor with a clang as a wide woman with breasts hanging unevenly down her stomach entered the room without a warning.

Chasing on her heels, the male servant holding the dinner tray rushed after her, telling her that she needed to knock.

The large woman stopped and stared at the mess in the room in stunned silence, letting the male servant push past her.

"Good afternoon, Fae Queen," he greeted and walked to the round table to put down the tray as evenly as he could between the rifts I had chopped onto it.

He didn't seem to want to acknowledge the destruction and instead bowed to Blake in greeting before his long legs propelled him out of the room.

"All Alpha lords be damned! What happened here?"

I flashed a timid smile at the woman, feeling my cheeks heat up.

"I've been practicing for the duel."

"How many wolves did you think you were fighting?"

She spun around in the room, her cyan eyes wide open as she studied the marks and cuts.

"One very fast and strong one," I answered, locking eyes with Blake.

She huffed loudly, shaking her head so her dark-brown curls bounced around her face. She tutted some more and appeared to get her wits about her as she folded out a black combat suit she was holding.

"See if this fits." She had barely handed it to me when she hit the bed like a storm, whipping off all the linen and balling it up in her arms. "And you!" She yelled at Blake. "Out with you!" She almost footed him in the butt, shepherding him on her way out.

After having everything up in the air, now the room was dead quiet. I didn't know what was worse. I could hear myself sigh. There was a smell of something green coming from the food tray; that was a good sign. This time there was only a cloche on the tray and I noticed that the wolf-head shaped knob was warm when I lifted the lid. A thick green soup was underneath and on the side there was a small plate with a bread roll accompanied by a small plate of butter and a knife, and a bowl of mixed fruits consisting of strawberries, blueberries and apple.

The creamy soup thickly coated the spoon as I dipped it in and I rolled it around my mouth, savouring the taste. There was potato, leek and I thought even a hint of asparagus. It was delicious.

I wanted to hate their food; wish that their way of living was much worse than the Fae way, but the chef had outdone Clarence by a mile. I devoured it so hastily it burned my tongue more than once but finished the fruits slowly. I dressed in my combat suit, happy to discover it was very stretchy. Bending and moving around to see its limits, I was suddenly startled by three gentle knocks on the door.

That is not the servant. Who then?

I hurried to the table, snatched up the knife and pushed it down into my boot. "Enter!" I shouted.

Blake poked his head in and entered slowly. He

looked so handsome in his formal Alpha heir wear; a white knee vest, a blue cape and a hefty belt where his sheath was hooked on.

He stood silently in the room staring at me for a while before he strode closer and closer. I saw suffering in his eyes and he sighed deeply as he pushed a strand of my hair behind my ear. His face came closer to mine.

Did he want to kiss me?

He opened his mouth slowly. "Roxie, it's time."

CHAPTER 20

I wasn't moving. I couldn't move. It took me a moment to breathe again.

It is time.

I would have preferred that wolf kiss rather than those words. My breath quivered as I inhaled. My father had warned me that the fear of the mind could weaken the body. He had trained me to be resilient to fear, but I had never been scared of him the way I was terrified of the Alpha.

I had been Daddy's girl and he would never have hurt me. Alpha Moon had no love for me and could easily make me look like an old dog-bitten soft toy with its stuffing ripped out between the seams.

I looked up at Blake and saw his eyes blank with his mind far away. He was stroking his hand over his mouth thoughtfully. It almost looked like he wanted to beg me to withdraw the challenge, but that would be scandalous. This was the moment I must show my worth.

I pulled the zip up the last bit of the collar on my battle suit as I cleared my throat.

"Are you taking me, or what?"

I gestured with my hand toward the door.

"Yeah, just…" He sighed kneeling down in front of me to buckle a leg strap with a small dagger around my thigh. "Stay low, Father hates to bend down when he fights because of a bad knee injury he suffered two years ago. He won't go for your face, so watch out for punches towards your ribs. He is right-handed, so stay away from the reach of his sword. Uhmm…he has a good heart, really, so don't make him angry, giving him any extra reasons to hate you. If he really unleashes his temper, not even the Fae Mother will be able to help you."

I looked at him. He seemed so sincere and in so much pain since the moment he'd heard me utter those words of the challenge.

Why was he helping me? Or was it all a bluff?

"Anything else?"

"Well, I was going to ask you whether you could make one of those yellow healing cords that I can hold on to until after the fight so that I can heal you with it?"

"No, you are not Fae," I snorted. "It doesn't work like that, as soon as I let it go, the cord will slowly start to disintegrate." I put a hand at my hip. "And besides, I'm not going to need healing."

He smiled, not believing that for one second and then he pushed the door wide open to let me pass him. He knew he had to take me but he still didn't seem settled.

"Is your ankle better?"

"What? How did you know that I had twisted my ankle?"

"I didn't. You're limping…very slightly."

"I'm not! I'm fine! I'm strong!"

He didn't argue, he only nodded, as he seemed to take in what I had said.

I passed him in the doorway, brushing up hard against him on purpose to show my authority.

He followed close behind me. "I'll take you to Helena first then."

"Who's Helena?"

And why had that made me jealous?

"She is my healer. If she assesses you before the fight, she might know how to treat you in any state you might be in after the duel."

"Sure you are not just delaying things?"

"I wish I could."

His answer took me aback. He really didn't want me to fight.

As I had halted, he took the lead and walked me outside and around the castle grounds. At the back there was a gravelled walkway leading up to a wooden hut with a thatched roof. The balustrade around the porch was made out of tree branches and the hut was almost impossible to detect, concealed behind pink flowered shrubs and lush foliage.

Blake pushed me up the steps to the porch as I hesitated. Two barn doors stood open, inviting us to enter. Inside, warm colours reflected on the walls from hundreds of candles scattered all around on shelves, tables and over the floor.

The place was rather romantic with a white sheet hung loosely over a bed, a large table against the side wall and two wooden chairs placed underneath the window.

A woman a few years younger than I, was standing by the table mixing herbs and plant leaves into a bowl. I could distinguish lavender, aloe vera, eucalyptus and rosemary at her side. Her face looked innocent behind the short brown hair that curtained at the sides of her cheeks.

"Helena!" Blake called.

She looked up with a sweet smile.

Blake pushed me forwards.

"This is Athroxane Crawford, Fae Queen of Fairola Kingdom."

Helena stopped grinding the ingredients around in the bowl and came to meet us.

"Pleased to finally meet you, Fae Queen; I've heard so much about you." She flashed Blake a knowing smile.

"Helena, the Fae Queen has challenged the Alpha to a duel."

"So I've heard. Brave."

"Stupid." Blake palmed his neck nervously.

"Hey!" I elbowed him in his stomach.

He closed his eyes, breathing steadily, seeming to ride out a sharp pain.

When he opened them again, he focused on Helena. "Can you see to her health? Make sure she doesn't die?"

"You don't make small requests, do you? She's going to fight the Alpha."

"Do what you can."

"I'll try." She waved at the bed with the white sheet. "Have a seat, sweetie." She turned to Blake. "And you! Outside!"

He hesitated, but reluctantly dragged his feet outside and one by one he swung the planked doors shut.

Helena approached the bed, her flowing white dress sweeping over the floor.

"Hold out your arm."

I held up my right arm towards her.

She clenched both her hands around my forearm a few times as if testing how strong my bones were.

"I don't know what advice to give you, my dear. All I can say is, if the Alpha breaks one of your bones, try to keep it straight so it heals straight. If he punctures a lung, try not to breathe so deeply and if you survive, don't moan to Blake about your pains."

Okay, those were not the health recommendations I had hoped for.

She went over to one of the candles on the floor and held her hands above the flame to warm them. "Lie down," she said, rubbing her hands together.

I swung my feet up, tensely flattening my spine against the bed and before I knew it, she was standing by the side of my bed again. The young woman's delicate fingers pulled down the zip of my battle suit and her hands escaped down my sides. She pressed and felt around in areas over my kidneys, my liver, my stomach and my uterus.

The way she did it made me feel that she really knew what she was doing, even though she was so young, and I was curious to know where she had obtained her tutoring. She pulled her hands out from my clothes and pushed her hair behind her ear before pressing it against my chest. I clenched my fists, tensing at the close contact and held my breath.

What is she doing?

I had a wolf girl lying with her head on the bulge of my breasts.

Surreal. Awkward.

"What will all this do to help me fight?"

"Nothing. I was just curious to know what only one heartbeat sounded like. I've never listened to a Fae heart before."

"If you listen closely, you'll hear it saying that you are too intrusive."

"Oh." Helena straightened up. "Sorry."

She carried on with her examination, pinching my skin and watching it sink back. "Yep, hydrated." She opened one of my eyes wide with her fingers. "Yep. White, not bloodshot." She felt my throat and glands. "Good. Say aaah."

I opened my mouth.

"Tongue looks healthy."

"So, all good?"

"Yep."

"Any other last advice?"

"If you ask me, I only have one advice; forfeit from the fight; lose your pride and keep your life."

"And shame the entire Fae Kingdom?"

"But!" she said abruptly holding a finger in the air. "Keep your life. Move on. Have a life somewhere else."

"Wolves are so weird."

"How come?"

"Wolves don't seem to respect honour. Blake has been telling me how to defeat his father and even provided me with this dagger." I said, pointing at my leg. "That's not normal."

"Oh that. Yeah well, he has had a crush on you since he was like five years old. The situation is agonising to him."

"What!" I leaned up on my elbows. "Why would you say that?"

"Blake talks a lot when he is coming back from being unconscious. And that has happened a lot. Bless him, he's a brave warrior, but devoid of regard for his own health."

"You're lying!"

"No, but there is someone else." She snapped her fingers, thinking. "Uhmm…Scratch or rather."

"Scratch?"

"Yes, he seemed to be the one you played with when the wolves visited the Fae Territory."

"Yes, but…" The fanfares bawled so loudly I almost fell off the bed. "What does that mean?"

"That's the invitation to the arena. They've opened the gates to let the spectators in."

It had begun.

My breath caught in my throat. Even more so when Blake stormed in and I was still half naked.

Demon Dogs!

I jumped out of bed and hurried to pull up the zip, hoping he hadn't seen anything. His panting breath was soon at my neck and I twisted to look up at him. His face had blushed crimson. He had definitely seen something he shouldn't.

"Please, reconsider." His voice was harsh.

At least now I knew why retiring from the duel was so important to him.

I snatched the sword he had provided for me out of his hand, buckling it on. "No!"

I was not going to reconsider anything! This fight was happening, and from what everyone had been telling me about the Alpha, I'd meet my match. If

Blake wanted this to end, he'd have to wait and watch the fight and see whether or not his father could kill me.

CHAPTER 21

My legs felt like lead as I walked to the arena. Blake was walking so close alongside me that I couldn't stretch out the entire length of my stride. He kept a protective arm around me in the same way as he kept a watchful eye all around us. A train of Blake's guards was in tow and some wolves were in front of us. Wolf shifters had come out of their houses and were lining the streets to look curiously at the fool who had challenged their leader. Through the open doors I could smell fresh bread, garlic and other herbs from dinners the families had recently enjoyed and which I would have rather attended than be walking towards my death.

The fanfare sounded once more. I looked up at Blake and met his carefully neutral expression.

He averted his gaze back to the myriad of spectators. "They are closing the gates. The arena is full."

Great! All of them wanted to come and see me be beaten to death.

My hold on the hilt became clammy and I clenched it harder. The balmy evening didn't help either. With my other hand I discretely rolled my fingers, working up a small blue cord but the cacophony of the gossip all around us made me constantly lose my focus.

"Did Helena fix your ankle?" Blake murmured into my ear.

"No. How could she do that?"

He didn't answer, just frowning heavily.

The closer we got to the tall curved building up ahead, the tighter the passage through the street became as more people crowded into the space around us.

"Keep clear!" Blake shouted at them at frequent intervals. They all stared at me like I was an already severely injured animal of prey that they could easily sink their fangs into.

All of them seemed to have dressed up for the occasion and they were all watching me from inside the hoods of their cloaks.

The large iron barred gates were closed when we arrived, but at the sight of us, three big guards forced one side ajar to let us in. I found myself encircled by a huge oval arena with no way out. Stone benches lined the sides, where cheering wolf shifters were standing up, obviously too excited by the event to remain seated. A stone floor made from many levelled boulders stretched toward a circular moat filled with water. In the centre of that circle was a raised plateau where I could see one figure standing, so I assumed the actual fighting ground was confined to that space.

Since the dimness of the evening had settled, candles and torches were lit in their thousands around the area amongst the seated. The crescent moon was glowing ominously in the green shaded sky above. Alpha Moon would have the advantage in this setting as I wasn't used to fighting at night.

Blake led me towards the ring, where blue-caped guards were preparing a gangplank to enable me to cross over the water. Blake held my hand in his steadily as I took my first steps onto the wobbly plank but then he had to let go and stay behind.

"Remember; stay low and guard your ribs."

His pleading eyes almost made my heart break as I edged away from him.

Alpha Moon stood in the middle of the battle ring waiting for me patiently, wearing a superior grin. The sparse clothes he wore showed that he didn't think the fight was going to be difficult. He had no armour, but only a pair of black leather trousers tucked into brown boots and nothing over his torso. He was playing with his sword, circling it in the air.

The moment I stepped off the gangplank it was pulled away, making me jump and I turned to look at the water surrounding us. To my horror, I now noticed spearheads sticking out, pricking through the surface.

So jumping in to swim across is out of the question.

Someone started to beat a drum whose sound echoed between the stone walls. I snapped my head back up to keep my eye on the Alpha; I had been momentarily distracted, looking back to the other side of the water where Blake was following the action with a careful eye.

I turned my head towards the Alpha again. He was closer now, walking with a confident playful stride.

How am I supposed to survive this? I'm shaking like a leaf.

I couldn't imagine my life getting any worse, but then I spotted the guard who had escorted me to my cell in Master Crowland's manor, standing amongst the crowd in the audience.

Great!

They had found me.

If Alpha Moon didn't kill me. Someone else stood in line to do it.

Alpha Moon stretched out his hand for me to shake it in honour of a fair fight. I swapped the sword to the other hand where I also held the blue cord and clutched his hand hard to try and convey that he had not intimidated me. He pulled me in close.

"I'll strike a few blows and then you stay down," he whispered into my ear.

Blake was right; he did have a good heart and wanted to spare me the pain and most of my pride. But I didn't want to lose any of it. All my enemies were watching and it could cost the Fae Kingdom greatly if I appeared weak.

As Alpha Moon was about to let go of my hand, I reeled him back in.

"If you forfeit now, I promise I won't kill you."

I stared him straight in the eye, hoping he might bend. His eyes closed as he let out an amused chuckle. I quickly switched the sword back to my right-hand and slammed my other palm with the button sized blue cord against his cheek. At impact we both screamed in pain; a sensation of ice zapped through my inside.

The audience gasped.

He shoved me to the ground as he stumbled backwards, pressing his hand onto the burn. I fell to my backside and slid across the stone ground, scraping my knees. Blood coated my skin and dropped down to my shin. My knees stung, but I had to get up fast. I had angered the Alpha; the one thing that Blake had warned me not to do and he would be coming after me for it.

When I glared back at him, he was turned towards the spectators as if someone there would be even angrier at the scar on his face than he was himself. I followed his line of sight to a balcony where his mate was sitting on a throne dressed in leather clothing decorated with chain-mail. She had her dark-brown hair braided tightly around her pale face and black paint lined horizontally across her eyes. It looked like her mouth had never smiled, her eyes had never sparkled with joy and her body had never relaxed. She sat straight like a stick with her arms hanging down, and with irritated fingers she was petting one of the three large grey wolves who were lying by her feet.

Alpha Moon returned to our fight and growled out the last bit of pain. His eyes had that look that I had seen before. He was angry, seeing red. He stalked across the ring, directly towards me. I avoided him, circling to the right, remembering that Blake had said he was right-handed. Although, he wasn't wearing any weapons what I could see, I almost wished he had, being beaten to death by his bare hands was going to be painful.

I held my sword up in front of me using both my

hands. Out of the corner of my eye, I could see Blake following me along the water's edge.

Clifford strode across the centre of the battle ring, approaching me fast. I swung the sword sharply through the air, hoping the blade could keep him at a distance but the Alpha didn't halt and swept his leg round in the air, kicking the sword clean out of my hands. I turned to see it vault across the rocks and beyond the edge, sinking down into the water.

It's gone.

I turned back to the wolf shifter but didn't have time to protect myself before the flat of his hand pounded on my chest. I was flung backwards, landing on my back and tumbling towards the edge of the moat, just stopping as one arm fell into the water. I gasped, seeing the spears under the surface up close. A whiff of the swampy water hit my nose.

Blake crouched down on the other side. "Stay down!" he hissed.

He obviously wanted me to lose so that I could help him steal the spell grimoire from the Courtess and break the curse. I hadn't believed a word Helena had said about Blake being a lovesick wolf in love with a Fae. It was all a part of the bluff.

I reached for my leg, pulling out the dagger from the leg strap. At the same time, I twisted my legs around and got up in one fluid movement. The strike hadn't subdued the Alpha's anger and he leaned in, swinging a punch at me. I leant backwards to avoid his fist and using the strength in my arms, managed a handstand, flipping my legs up in the air and kicking the Alpha in the face. As I landed down on my knees again, my fingers throbbed where they had been squashed to the ground under the dagger handle in the acrobatics.

The Alpha's cheek looked red and irritated and he stood still now, probably waiting for me to get up. What Blake had told me about him not liking to bend down appeared to be true. But he wasn't going to wait forever.

I continued to circle to my right, ready to slice him with my dagger if he attacked.

He didn't follow but dug into his pocket to bring something out. He brought his hand through his hair to catch the top layer of his shoulder-length hair and tie it into a knot at the top of his head, making his dark eyebrows and his three-day stubble more prominent.

Maybe that was a good sign. He must have realised this fight wasn't going to be as easy as he had thought; maybe he'd thought I would stay down.

He ran towards me at full pelt and my heart raced harder than a stampeding herd of wild horses. I held my hands up in front of me in order to defend myself with the dagger but he avoided it by throwing himself on the ground and kicked out behind him, striking me behind my kneecaps. I was too slight of build to be any match for his brute strength, and his strike felled me, the back of my head banging hard against the cobbles.

My ears were ringing from the blow to my head but I could just make out the muffled sound of the audience cheering.

Okay, so he can fight bending down.

I reached up to check whether I was bleeding but had no time before Clifford footed me in the ribs.

How dirty. I'm lying down.

Quickly, I rolled away from him and stumbled to

my feet. My vision was swimming and blurred and all I could see was a ghost of a figure approaching. I had no protection having lost my dagger in my fall.

This time, he kicked higher up. I ducked swiftly, and by a lucky chance found the dagger on the ground so I grabbed it and stabbed it into the back of his thigh.

He roared. The spectators cried out in sympathy.

Clifford yanked the dagger out and tossed it to one side. He came at me again; not even limping. I was still on my knees and unable to move away fast enough before his fist hit my face.

Blake had said he wouldn't go for the face! Liar!

I fell with my arm trapped under my own weight, but just managed to roll to one side to avoid his next blow. The powerful punch struck the ground. He grunted, his knuckles bloodstained.

He threw himself over me like he was grabbing for a cockroach, lifting me up high with a tight grip around my throat.

I clawed at his hand, struggling to breathe and the pain that radiated from my throat to my head was excruciating. The Alpha turned me around as if he was holding up the match trophy, to display me to the audience. When he finally stopped, I was facing Blake who was holding his hand over his eyes. I lifted my knee and found the lining of my boot where I fished out the table knife I had hidden there since supper. I jammed it hard into Clifford's armpit.

He roared and let me go, flapping around with his other arm to reach the knife and pull it out of his flesh. Now, he had two puncture holes that were bleeding hard. If I could keep it up like this, I only needed to wait for him to faint from the blood loss.

He rolled his shoulder, it looked like the wound was finally bothering him as he clutched at his bulging biceps.

He shook his head. "You have the same respect for wolves as your father."

"Do not speak about my father. Murderer!"

"Murderer?" Clifford stopped in his step. "He was trapped under a boulder, how was that my fault?"

I didn't know the answer to that, why the war had started, or why they had been fighting one another. I edged myself closer to the bloodied dagger which Clifford had removed from his thigh earlier and crouched down to pick it up.

"Lose the blades, shall we?" Clifford prompted, indicating that he was ready to drop the one he was holding.

I shook my head frantically. The dagger was the best chance I had of winning.

"Fine then." The Alpha barged towards me.

I stuck the blade out just as he came close, but he blocked my arm with his wounded one and used his left to slice at my waist. I cried out as I felt a sharp sting on my flesh and blood oozed out from a rip in my battle suit. The next sting was on my thigh. I bent over reflexively to press my hand against the cut, but as I did the Alpha kneed me in the face. I dropped to the ground, squirming from the pain in my bleeding nose. Tears welled out of my eyes blinding me even though I wasn't crying.

"Stay down!" Blake called out.

No way was I going to give up. I tried to get up on my knees but received a kick to my ribs that seemed to knock every bit of breath from my body. I lay gasping for air, enduring the worst pain I had ever felt. I tried to get up once more but his foot slammed into my stomach again and again. Heat throbbed through me as my own body was trying to repair the damage.

"Get up!" he bawled, stamping on my knee so hard I was sure he broke the bone.

Moments later, he lifted me slightly off the ground by my collar and delivered several fist punches against my head. Warm liquid ran down my face.

I was in so much pain.

I wish I could die already!

I was dropped to the ground and my head bobbed to the side. On the other side of the water I could see Blake backing up and sprinting towards the battle ring, jumping over the moat.

Was he insane? If he hadn't had made it all the way over, he would have been speared!

"Enough!" he growled loudly towards his father, placing himself between us.

All the wolf shifters in the stands gasped, but after that it was soundless; no chatter, no whisper, just complete silence.

"Blake, you know the code of the duel. She challenged me!"

"She is defeated. There is nothing more to prove."

"Son, get out of my way."

My vision was fading in and out, and I only saw in black and white. Parts of their conversation were muted and I felt as if I was letting go of life. There was no light coming for me, only a darkness that consumed me.

Gentle fingers stroked my neck. "She is really

bad." I heard Helena say, but I couldn't see her.

What was she doing in the ring?

"Both of you leave now, and Helena, you are not allowed to heal her. I'm going to make sure everyone knows what happens to those who challenge the Alpha."

CHAPTER 22

The light started glowing yellow inside my eyelids, but then it disappeared. I felt the weight of my body, but then I was floating. It went dark...

I heard hushed voices, but then they went silent. I took a breath, detecting my heart beat. It went dark...

There was pain. The pain lessened. It increased worse than before. It went dark...

I was dizzy, but I could open my eyes. White curtains danced in the wind seeping through the window. Sunlight streamed in and landed to warm my arm. I recognised this place. It was the healing hut. I looked down to see I was covered with a white sheet, all but my bare arms and my chest.

I'm naked!

There was a weight at my feet. I lifted my head up and saw there was a wolf lying curled up at the foot of the bed. Blake.

Of course, it's daytime. The wolf curse.

Slowly, I recalled the duel.

I'm alive.

Blake had interfered. He had saved my life. Most likely he had majorly dishonoured his father and the reputation of the Alpha family by stopping the duel and sparing the life of a Fae.

He stretched out on the bed, moving his head backwards to lay his chin on my knees, looking at me with his dark green eyes. They looked sad and he whined softly. Instinctively, I wanted to pet him. I'd had both pet and guard dogs around the castle when I was growing up that looked very similar to him, but there was a grown man inside this one; one who understood me and could talk to me at night time.

I twisted my head to the right as I heard scraping noises. Helena approached us, grinding a pestle and mortar.

"I would say, good evening, Fae Queen, but yours has definitely been rough."

She was wearing the same white dress as the day before but now it was splotched all over with dry blood. Her eyes looked bloodshot as if she hadn't slept and her hair was escaping from its previously immaculate ponytail.

She smudged a green paste from her mortar over a large scar I had across the left side of my chest.

I put a hand up to scratch my head and discovered a large spiralling bandage in the way.

"What happened?"

"The Alpha beat the crap out of you, and I'm trying to put you back together again."

"I remember. I lost the duel. Well, at least I

survived."

"Technically, you died. Blake…"

Blake swiftly rolled over to his stomach and barked at Helena.

Helena stared at him with a sceptical look. "You are not going to tell her?"

Blake growled and lowered his jaw to the mattress.

"Fine. Your choice, but I will tell you 'I told you so' when the shit hits the fan."

"What?" I asked.

"That's between you and Blake now."

I looked at him. He twisted his head more to avoid my eyes.

I looked back at Helena. "I heard that Clifford forbade you from healing me. Isn't it dangerous for you to disobey him?"

She shrugged her shoulders. "What the Alpha doesn't know…but a burning at the stake would be the punishment if he found out."

"Holy Fae Mother! Why did you do it then!"

"Blake asked me to."

I was stunned. What had they done?

I heard another whine from the end of the bed.

I stayed quiet, breathing heavily and with my head full of thoughts.

Helena gently massaged the paste over my chest. She too, was quiet and I felt awkward. Not many people had seen me without the court furs and wigs, and definitely not this naked; she was studying every piece of my skin like I was a delicate flower. She seemed so calm even though she had just signed her death warrant to help Blake.

"So, for how long have you been in love with

Blake?" I asked.

She smiled. "You know he hears you, right?"

I looked down to the foot of the bed. His ears flicked, listening.

"And I'm afraid your assumption is entirely misguided," she giggled, carrying on with her healing massage. "I have always been in love with a fantasy. Blake has told me so many stories about you that I fell in love with the idea of you. Your beauty, your intelligence and bravery – not that the real you is any less glorious."

Sensually, she coated the grass-like paste onto the edge of my lip with her thumb.

I didn't know what to focus on; the fact that Blake had said all those nice things about me or that a woman was trying to seduce me.

I cleared my throat. "So, you like women?"

She shook her head. "Doesn't matter to me what gender you are, if I like the way you make me feel, I can fall in love. I grew up learning that love is good and hate is bad – it's that simple. Love doesn't have a gender, colour or age, it's just good."

I don't know why I let her carry on touching my face but with the pain I was suffering, her strokes were comforting.

I closed my eyes and let a pleasurable moan escape.

Suddenly, the weight on my feet shifted and Blake barked. I opened my eyes. He stared at Helena before limping up to sniff the paste on my face with his cold nose making wet punctuations on random places.

"Yes, Blake, it's the quality stuff. The ointment I used on you when you fought off the grizzly bear at

Jungle Cove." Helena pushed Blake down toward my feet again. "And I'll give you a tub to take with you on your way."

"On my way?"

"To retrieve the grimoire. You can't stay here. We don't want anyone to find you in my care. You know...the burning on stake punishment."

"Oh, of course."

I turned my head, discovering the doors were shut.

How long did I have until the guards found me? I couldn't go on a treasure hunt yet, all of me ached and my chest rasped as I breathed.

"But the guards must know you brought me here." I leaned up. "I have to go."

My head throbbed as I struggled to sit up, and the cut on my side stung.

"Not so fast, Fae Queen. Everyone saw you die. No one is looking for you; Alpha Moon believes that Blake buried you last week. You still have a score to settle with Blake though." She looked at him meaningfully. "He will smuggle you out tonight after dark."

"Last week! How long have I been unconscious for?"

"You were in and out of consciousness for ten days. The first three days you really had me worried."

Ten days! Dead!

Everyone thought I was dead and that meant Master Crowland too. This was my chance to hide away from the world and no one would know I was alive. I could start afresh and if there was to be an accident on the road and Blake died, I wouldn't have to go on a wild goose chase to figure out how to reverse the blood curse. Only Helena would know I was alive and she wouldn't tell anyone and risk being burned at the stake. But what about Scratch, I couldn't just leave him imprisoned here. I would have to come back to set him free.

I lay back down again. I had to sleep more if I was going to travel all night. It wouldn't be hard to fall asleep, I was exhausted and Helena was singing a sweet tune as she walked about the room preparing things. My eyes became heavier and heavier as I let my eyelashes rest on my cheeks.

I had almost drifted off when a boom at the doors, loud enough to make the planks creak and splinter, made me almost jump out of my skin.

What was that?

There was another boom, making the planks bend inwards and I could see something made out of wood in between the cracks.

My heart started tapping faster in an unrecognisable beat. Blake flew to his paws on top of the bed, growling and barking menacingly towards the door. His lips receded, exposing long and sharp fangs.

Another shove at the door and a wooden wolf head broke through a hole.

A battering ram?

The glass bowl that Helena was holding slipped out of her hands and smashed to the floor, shattering into a thousand pieces. She looked petrified as we both stared at a beefy arm that had shot in through the gap in the broken door and yanked away the beam that had been acting as a barricade.

Blake jumped down from the bed, placing himself between us and the doors, ready to defend us.

The doors were flung open and a group of

guards stormed in followed by an extremely pissed-off looking Alpha Moon in wolf form. The hair on his back stood on end, all his fangs were displayed and his eyes were almost poisonous to look at. The Alpha crept a step closer to Helena, snapping at her form, which triggered Blake to lope towards him, thrusting his face up close to his father's. Alpha Moon tried to walk around him, but Blake growled and followed his every move.

As they stared at each other, the group of guards stood bewildered in the doorway. The first guard seemed to regain his focus and tapped on the shoulder of the guard behind him and then indicated at me.

Blake was clearly out of options. He couldn't protect both of us from all of them and as a result he attacked his father. A ferocious fight broke out. The two wolves moved so quickly that both of them blended into a blur and when they paused, growling at one another, both had blood coating their teeth.

Blake pounced on his father once again but his father fought back as though there was no humanity inside him, just an animal lashing out to kill.

The last rays of the sun that had been shining in through the window disappeared, changing day to night. The two wolves instantly transformed and backed away from each other. Alpha Moon dried the blood off his mouth with his arm.

"Guards, grab him!" He pointed at his son.

The head guard left my bedside and advanced towards Blake.

"Do you want me to lock him up in his room, Alpha?"

"No," Clifford grunted. "I want him to watch

this. Maybe he will learn his place in *my* pack."

Two of the guards pulled Blake's arms behind his back with difficulty as Blake twisted and squirmed, trying to free himself.

"Father, don't do this. I beg this of you."

"Wolves who have disobeyed me beg for mercy all the time, you are no exception. The wolf laws stand. Take her!"

Two of the other blue-caped guards seized Helena and led her out of the hut after Blake.

"No! Don't touch her! Let her go! What will you do to the Queen?" Blake was shouting as they manhandled him until his voice ebbed out in the distance.

Alpha Moon still stood staring at me with four remaining guards at his back. He was looking at me as if he was contemplating whether to kill me quickly, or torment me slowly.

CHAPTER 23

"You!" the Alpha said angrily, pointing at me. "I'll deal with later." He turned on his heel and walked out between the four guards who parted down the middle.

Their blue capes were flying wildly around them, covering any sight I had of the outside through the obliterated doorway.

I dug my face into my hands.

What will they do to Helena now?

Somehow, I had to try and stop them from punishing her. She had saved *my* life, but I was in so much pain that I didn't know how I would even be able to stand.

Just touching the raw scabs, which were trying to heal in every corner of my face, hurt like hell. Yet, I couldn't give up. I had to manage, by advancing one step at a time.

First, I needed my clothes. I looked around to find them hanging over the back of one of the chairs under the window.

So, my first challenge is to get there.

I circled my foot under the sheet.

Ouch! That's painful.

I bit my teeth together and slowly sat up, each bend of the skin and pull of the muscles hurting. Once I had managed to sit, I breathed out and took a new lungful of air before I lifted each leg over the edge of the bed. My ears started to drum inside my aching head.

Shit! How will I manage this!

I eased my feet down onto the floor, sensing every toe bend as I rolled my whole foot flat onto my heel.

Oooooo!

I breathed out.

With my hand I pushed my backside off the bed, shifting gravity, feeling it weighing down my spine.

Okay, I can stand.

It was painful but grimacing was even more so, stretching the sores in my face. I limped towards the chair, sitting down gently, and twisting back to grab my battle suit. Putting up with the agony, I bent down to pull each leg on in turn.

I was never going to make it there like this.

I stood up, softly inserting my arms into the sleeves. The suit was stiff in places from dried blood. My own blood. There were large rips in the fabric too which had not yet been mended. I slid my feet into the dirty boots and didn't tie them as tight as usual. I undid the bandage around my head and put my hair up in a loose bun. It probably didn't look great, but I wasn't going to put my arms up above my head more than necessary.

Okay, ready.

I motioned myself forward, building up a swaying momentum to get out onto the porch and hobble down the steps. I looked up as I saw black smoke spiralling into the sky in the opposite direction to the arena; the acrid air noticeable even at this distance.

I couldn't see any guards near the gates so I hurried out, as much as I was able. I followed the dark smoke towards a large grassy hill, making sure I was staying away from the open road. There was increasing commotion the closer I got towards the hill top. People were shouting, wolves were howling and I could hear flames crackling.

I made my way up the hill, crawling in the long grass for the last bit, careful not to be spotted as I peered over the edge. The bonfire in front of me was huge, the flames reaching up to the treetops as they danced over the twigs. Tied to a pole at the top of the pile was Helena. She tossed and turned, trying to loosen her hands from the rope and at the same time she shouted: "Love is good, hate is bad."

Alpha Moon was sitting on his throne on a raised platform next to his wife, ignoring Helena's message. Blake had been forced to his knees in front of his parents by a large blue-cape. The guard was pinning Blake's head under his arm so tightly that Blake's face had turned red; his eyes directed so that he had a clear view of what was going on - forced to watch Helena burn.

There was no way I could climb that mountain of burning logs at the best of times. With my injuries and having to fight off guards at the same time, it would be impossible for me to save her.

The fire rose quickly and was encircling Helena's feet. She started screaming with panic in her voice.

"Father!" Blake shouted pleadingly, but from what I could see, it just looked like the guard pressed Blake's jaw harder together.

A woman with long black hair and dressed in a brown coat with a fur along the collar was crying hysterically as she threw herself onto her knees in front of the Alpha. I couldn't hear what she was saying, but I didn't have to. This was a desperate mother begging for her daughter's life.

The flames caught onto Helena's bloodstained white dress and started to eat on her bare feet, making them turn black. She screamed even louder, an ear-splitting sound I was never going to be able to forget.

I folded my arms on the grass and buried my face in them.

I can't watch this.

I was a queen but had no powers here to do anything. Only when the cacophony of voices had died down and the horrendous grieving cry from the mother ebbed away, did I peer up again. I couldn't see Helena. She had turned into a pile of ash on a bed of charcoal. The spectators had cleared out and the Alpha family was rising and preparing to leave with a dozen blue-capes at their heels.

The guard holding Blake finally released him, dropping him like a puddle to the floorboards of the royal podium. Blake shouted out in grief without any signs that he planned to stand up. Everyone left, but Blake was still lying on his front, raising his chest off the floor to watch the pile where Helena had been.

When I couldn't hear or see anyone else, I crawled to my feet and crossed the hillside to get closer to Blake. He was hiding his face into his arm when I arrived. I put my hand gently on his shoulder but he didn't flinch or look up. He seemed utterly devastated.

"Blake, I'm so sorry."

He stopped breathing when he heard my voice and slowly sat up, trying to hide his grief.

"Thank you. She was a very good friend." He dried his nose on his sleeve. "She died screaming in agony."

I felt my heart breaking for him. "Yes, I know. I saw it."

He sighed. "How're you feeling?"

I looked up at the pile of burnt wood, whose ambers were still glowing in places.

"I can't complain."

He looked forwards as well. "No, I guess not."

He inhaled a deep breath, looking up at the full moon. I bet he missed being able to howl at it.

He stood up, stretching down a helping hand towards me.

"Come on, we need to leave. I don't want you to be next."

"Where will we go?"

"Helena sacrificed her life to heal you so that you could help break the blood curse, and you lost the duel, you're not going to back away from your word now, are you? We need to get the grimoire."

"You're going to keep digging my grave, pushing me into a deeper hole than I'm already in?"

"Queens get a nicer grave than a hole, they normally burn at sea." He tried to smile cheekily.

"Fine. I am a queen and a woman of my word. But when the Courtess catches us trying to steal the grimoire and wants to add your fur to her wardrobe, don't blame me."

"No," he said, fetching his sword that had been leaned against the throne and shoving it back into the sheath. "We are going to ask for a hearing with the Fae Council."

"What?" I stared at him but could not see any hesitation or insincerity. "Are you serious?"

"I'm serious. We are doing this the right way from now on. Get up and let's go!"

"Now? You're crazy. We can't do that. They'll kill me!"

"I'm sure they are more civilised than the Alpha."

"No! I won't go. They might not burn me but I don't feel like being sacrificed to the Fae Mother for my sins."

"I won't let that happen."

"Won't let that happen? Like you were able to protect Helena?"

His eyes widened and his nostrils flared. "I won't make the same mistake twice."

I knew he meant well, but I also knew my guards' ambitions. I shook my head. "You won't be able to stop them from taking me and killing you."

"If they kill me, they kill me, I feel dead anyway with this curse. You're coming with me to get permission from the Fae council to lift it, even if I have to drag you there."

CHAPTER 24

I didn't want to accept his hand, which was still stretched toward me to help me off the ground. I wanted to run, but I couldn't - I was in too much pain. He had been right about me not being able to beat Alpha Moon, and I wouldn't get far trying to flee from Blake either. He was heartbroken and angry, and it was doubtful that he would be susceptible to negotiations at this point.

He flicked with his hand in the air in front of me, prompting me to take it. "Come, there is something I want to show you."

I clasped it irritably and slowly stood up but then quickly let go. He turned to walk out onto the wide grassy field beyond the hill, in the opposite direction from where all the spectators had exited. A frightened deer scurried off as we passed by and I saw one or two rabbits nibbling on dandelion leaves in the dark, but other than that, it was quiet. After we had walked a while, some crickets started stroking their legs, but Blake was still striding over the damp grass in silence. I admired the stars glowing above us and the full moon reminded me of the promises I had made to lift the blood curse.

Blake led me into the dark forest at the far edge of the field; the city behind us was now only a foggy line on the horizon. I could see a cottage between the trees, with light glowing out of the windows and someone was moving inside it. My heart started pounding. I turned to Blake. "Who lives here?"

"This cottage is not fit to live in, but I think you'll be happy to see who is hiding in it. But first, follow me around the back."

I wasn't sure I understood what was going on but neither did I believe I had a choice, I sneaked up close behind him, prepared for anything which could be jumping out of the dark. Around the corner a pair of yellow eyes stared our way. I shrank back but Blake kept going.

"Are you not going to say hello to an old friend?" Blake questioned me mischievously.

I took another few careful steps forward, and when the creature moved in the dark and snorted, I was overjoyed.

"Mazzi!"

Had I been well, I would have jumped the fence to get to her but in my state I could only jog up close and stretch out my hand to my loving mare. She seemed equally happy to see me and pushed her head close to caress mine.

Blake lined himself up to me, supporting his arms on the fence and stroked Mazzi's neck.

I glanced at him, still keeping my forehead on Mazzi's blaze.

"How did you find her?"

"I'm a wolf who has all day to kill."

I wanted to thank him but I just couldn't. My sores were too raw to think about forgiveness for everything I had gone through and he had to settle for a thankful smile.

I could see two more horses behind Mazzi, grazing on the long grass.

"Three horses?"

That playful smile that I hadn't seen in a long while was back on his lips. He didn't answer as we heard the cottage door creak open and then a thump as it closed.

Blake flashed another quick smile at me before turning around. "Ready to go?"

I looked at the man coming around the corner who Blake had addressed.

Scratch leaned arrogantly with his shoulder on the wall of the cottage. "On the Queen's command."

"Scratch!"

I dragged myself towards him to get caught up in his embrace. His strong arms making me cry out softly in pain. He took a step back, catching my chin and tilting my head to one side. Anger filled his eyes.

"What have you done to her?"

He inspected my sores intently.

Didn't he know what had happened?

Blake placed himself firmly next to Scratch, glancing sorrowfully at me. "She challenged the Alpha."

Scratch looked stunned and blinked with big eyes. "You did what?"

I snatched my chin away from his grip. "It was the only way to buy back my freedom."

"And you're alive?"

Blake snorted. "Not because she won. She didn't."

Scratched looked confused.

I became increasingly annoyed, placing my hand at my hip. "Blake's healer worked wonders but now she is dead because of it."

"Roxie," Blake sighed. "That's not your fault. It was mine and now I'm going to make it right."

"Roxie?" Scratch huffed glowering at Blake. "You should use her appropriate title."

"I meant no disrespect, Fae Queen. Let's saddle up and get going towards the Fae Court before it turns morning and I turn wolf."

"The Fae Court!" Scratch gasped.

"Yes," I sniggered. "Blake wants to ask them for help."

"But they will kill Queen Athroxane. That's not the deal we struck when you got me from the dungeons. You said we were going to fight to reinstate her on the throne."

"Yes, by strengthening her relationship with the court members. They are powerful Fae who she will need to have at her back. Fighting them won't help."

"Yes, it will. Surely, she will have the support of the guards and they will be at her disposal. They know her as their rightful queen."

"So, you want her to start her reign with an open battle against her council?"

"If that's what it takes."

"And if it doesn't have to come to that?"

"Okay, fine." Scratch paced a few steps back and

forth. "If they agree to meet at the border of the wolf territory to discuss how their nation shall be ruled in the future, we go peacefully. If not, we fight for her rights. Agreed?"

"Agreed. Good, because I've already sent out a scout with a message for them to meet us."

I stood gobsmacked as the men bickered over how I should live my life.

"Do I get a say in this?"

Instantly, both men turned my way and shouted, "No!"

Offended, I pressed my lips together.

The way Scratch's muscles tensed, I thought he was prepared to punch Blake at this point, but instead he stomped towards a rickety outhouse and swung the door up so hard it came right off its hinges. He grunted unapologetically, tossing it to the ground on one side. Three backpacks and three saddles were on the floor inside the outhouse. He picked up one of the saddles and with large, hurried strides he went over to open the gate of the horse's paddock.

"Are you guys coming?"

Blake snapped out of his defensive stance and fetched the other two saddles. "I'll saddle Mazzi. I don't want you to exert yourself," Blake muttered when he passed me, walking towards the enclosure. "We must leave the Skyland territory as soon as possible. Father will have wolves tracking us as soon as he realises that Athroxane is missing."

He saddled Mazzi first. She allowed it without any fuss, seeming to have taken a liking to him. He carried on to saddle another black gelding before picking up the backpacks, handing one out to me.

"It has everything you'll need for a week."

Scratch intercepted, snatching the bag out of his hand.

"She can't carry that weight. I'll do it."

"I wasn't planning for her to have it on her back; we'll strap it to Mazzi's rear but she will need it in case we lose one another. No one knows what will happen in the woods, and frankly, I don't trust you. The king would still be alive today if the green capes hadn't attacked us at the Wolf Temple."

What? Was Blake trying to put the blame on the green capes now?

I saw what happened. Alpha Moon is the one who should shove his tail between his legs.

"If your father hadn't kept me captive, the green capes wouldn't have attacked."

"True. We could have settled it in a more civilised manner, that's all I am saying."

"Look at the Fae Queen!" Scratch screamed at him, pointing at me. "Look at her state! You call that civilised?"

"Guys!" I shouted over them both and they turned to look at me. I bent my knee and wiggled my leg behind me. "Who wants to help me up."

Both reacted at the same time, but Scratch pushed Blake back. "I think you've done enough."

Scratch hoisted me up and as I swung my leg over the saddle, I wanted to cry my eyes out; the aches were so bad. I bit my teeth together and breathed deeply until the worst of the pain had subsided.

By the time I looked up again, both men had mounted too.

Scratch seemed to observe me. "Why don't you make a healing cord to remove the pain?"

"I just haven't had the time. It takes a while to do it."

He nodded, seeming to agree with that. "You set the speed, Fae Queen," Scratch said as he lined himself up next to me.

A trot was all the rocking I could manage. As I rode, I looked up to let the stars guide my way and steered Mazzi towards the south. I loved the sway of Mazzi's walk, it was a familiar feel in all this craziness; her clopping hooves, her puffing snorts and her warm grey fur, I revelled in it all.

All that comfort disappeared though when I heard a snapping noise, like a branch breaking, deeper into the woods and I remembered all my hardships. There were so many who wanted me dead and Blake and Scratch were leading me towards some of them right this very moment. I didn't want to see Jarminne's ugly mug ever again, but frankly, I didn't want to steal the grimoire from the Courtess either, so the only other option I had in order to avoid both of those circumstances was to flee north as far as north went and live in solitude in the wilderness.

Scratch rode up next to me, offering me water. I couldn't reject, I was desperate to quench my thirst, but it also bothered me that he was so extremely watchful, guarding me closely. I needed some space to be able to sprint away and get a head start, if I was going to be able to outrun both men and Blake's horse, which looked particularly strong.

New hope entered my heart when I felt a wind sweeping by, cooling my cheek. A short distance away the moist soil offered the perfect conditions to bring about mist. It was a cold night, so only a few minutes from now I should be able to flee into a thick layer of cloud. I would make sure they weren't able to find me, and I would be free – not a queen any more, but alive and free!

I waited until we had gone a bit further and the mist had started to rise, swirling around the horse's hooves before I plucked up the courage to initiate my plan, even though I was still scared of what they would do to me if they caught me again. Perhaps they would tie me up and I would have to ride in front of Blake again. My cheeks warmed at the thought which took me by surprise. I shook the feeling off.

I was going to risk it. My heart started pounding faster.

Gosh, I'm nervous.

This was it.

Discretely, I tapped with my heels at Mazzi's sides and as ever, she reacted instantly.

It was now or never.

I used all my remaining might to work her into motion, increasing speed rapidly towards the denser mist that would be my cloak of invisibility.

"Athroxane!"

"Roxie!"

Scratch and Blake called after me, and I could hear them take up chase.

I'd rather die than be caught. Come on, Mazzi, faster!

A sharp prick stung at my neck. I lifted my hand up to feel around and got hold of some feathers.

A poison dart.

Now, even the mist became blurry, and I heard the clanging of metal. Blake and Scratch were fighting something. They were shouting, but to me their words were too vague.

Dizzy and nauseous, I slowly slumped down

onto Mazzi's back. I wasn't following her swaying anymore, as my body was bouncing limply in the saddle.

Who had come? What was happening?

I could only see mist and dark clothes. Someone rode up alongside me and pulled me over onto their horse, laying me in front of them on my stomach before setting off at a gallop. I was taken towards the west and not back to Skyland City, Master Crowland's manor, or towards Fairola Kingdom.

Where was I being taken?

CHAPTER 25

Thump...thump...thump. I palmed my forehead.
Gosh, what a headache.

I rubbed the sleep out of my eyes and looked around in the room.

Where am I?

The room was dark. A blue tinted light glowed in through the window, between the thick curtains, enabling me vaguely to make out the décor in the room. The space before me had dark wooden panelling along the bottom half of the walls with the top in a dark-teal colour. The rustic four-poster bed placed on a beige and red rug, was neatly thatched with flowery engravings. On either side of the bed, matching nightstands featured tall lamps with sturdy golden feet. Above my head, two paintings were framed in gold and depicted the Fae Court from different angles.

Whoever lived here must at least like Fae, although that wasn't to say I counted. I uncovered myself from the blanket and gently lifted my legs off the bed.

I'm wearing a white nightgown.

My skin was clean. I smelt my forearm and it had a soft hint of coconut. I pinched a strand of hair and sniffed eucalyptus. It was all so odd that I feared I was indulging in false hope, but I certainly was being treated like a queen.

Someone has cared for me. Who?

I rushed to the window and looked out, but could only see trees. I yawned and stretched. It seemed I needed to peer out through the door to find out more so I carefully tip-toed towards the door and stopped to listen for voices.

There was silence.

I grabbed the handle and yanked it down to open the door ajar. The brightest blue eyes were trying to peek between the gap to look back at me.

A Beetle Guard.

I shut the door.

If the Courtess's guards were posted outside my room, it must mean I was in her mansion.

I shrugged.

When I was a child, I always used to hide when the Courtess came to visit the castle with her guards in tow. The Beetle Guards terrified me; their tall helmets with tentacles sticking out and their armour was shaped like an angry beetle's. Their armguards were lined with jagged iron all the way out to their golden sharp claws. The baldric held a sword as large as themselves with a jagged blade and a hilt sprawling with six legs, making my skin crawl. The Beetle

Guards didn't wear trousers, their chain-mail skirt clanked as they walked, layered with a blood-red fabric underneath sections of crafted iron plates.

That was the noise I now heard receding further and further away. Had the guard left his post?

I poked my head out once more to look. Five guards just outside my room turned their heads to look at me, making me feel like I had stepped my foot into a beetle nest.

I closed the door. My heart was pounding.

I was heavily guarded. Why? What could I do now?

Climb out the window. Yes, I should do that.

I put my hands on the windowsill leaning in to inspect the opening mechanism. There was a small metal sash lock. I fingered over it to flick the lever to the side before pushing up the frame halfway. Normally, I would probably have done a forward roll to jump out the window, but with my pains, I eased up to sit on the sill instead and gently lifted out one leg then the other until I was sitting poised to jump.

Suddenly, the door opened and I turned my head back so fast that the ailments in my neck got even worse. Two Beetle Guards marched in and abruptly turned to their side to allow Courtess Flamirna to enter the room. The two guards behind her, lined up next to the first two. She walked towards the bed, but stopped and clasped her hands in front of her when she saw me climbing out of the window.

Chills ran down my arm as she looked at me; her white face expressionless. She was wearing her official black court gown and a teardrop mountain crystal was stuck between her black brows. Her long white hair was parted on either side of her pointy ears, which were fully clad with jewels.

"You will probably encounter more dangers out there than in here, my Queen."

She wasn't stopping me from escaping; she only stood waiting for my response.

"You're not going to kill me?"

"Wouldn't dream of it, my Queen. I came for you as soon as I heard you were still alive. I mourn your father still."

"Thank you, Courtess. I thought you were going to execute me for fleeing the battlefield."

"I know you didn't. You were pushed away from it. Although, the court bailiff are far harder to convince."

"How do you know all of this?"

"I have eyes and ears everywhere."

The Courtess seemed to have stopped smiling many years ago, but she instilled such serenity that I dared climb back inside.

"I have made all the necessary arrangements to prepare our army for retaliation to avenge your father. They are ready for your instructions."

"No!"

"No? My Queen?" Her brows lowered.

"I don't want to attack them."

"But, my Queen, I have to insist you take advice from your council. Not to strike back is a sign of weakness and it emphasises the signs of your betrayal to our race. If you make such a statement, I fear I can't protect you from your council."

"There will be no war!"

"I don't understand. Make me see the reason for your choice."

"Father placed a blood curse on the Alpha family

and I have given my word that I am going to help them reverse it."

The Courtess took a shocked step back. "You want to help the wolves? But…the late king…"

Her light-green eyes gleamed with worry.

I thought back to how much Blake had helped me. I had so desperately wanted to flee north, but confessing out loud to the Courtess had made me realise it was only fair that I kept my word.

"I have already made my promises."

"I doubt anyone in the Fairola Kingdom would blame you for not upholding your word when you had to make it whilst being held captive."

She had a point. I had been forced into it, but hearing the torturing screams of Helena just made it feel right to honour her death. She was the biggest victim in all this, but so had my father been and all those soldiers who had died during the wolf attack. I had many more reasons that supported the choice of protecting my own people rather than just keeping my word to an Alpha who had nearly killed me.

I felt torn. On the one hand, helping the wolves was the only way to avoid war and it was what my father would have wanted. He'd taught me that keeping your word was important, to show your integrity as a role model for how you wanted your people to behave. Why should they have integrity if the queen doesn't? he used to say. However, if I helped the wolves, my own Fae people would rise up against me. This was my chance to break my promises to the Alpha and go back home to live happily ever after in luxury.

I sunk down on the bed. My choice seemed impossible to make.

"What are your orders, my Queen?"

I inhaled a deep breath. "Summon the court for a hearing."

"As you command. I will have you escorted back to the castle so you can prepare. This time, *you* will be sitting on the First Throne."

My heart did a double take. Of course, I was queen now and I was entitled to sit on my father's chair – the First Throne. I had heard the jargon of court communication many times, but never had the need to use it personally. There was normally never only one matter to discuss in a court hearing so it might mean that I had to make real decisions in other disputes as well. I felt my knees weaken with the dawning thought.

"What happened to Blake and Scratch in the woods, by the way?"

"We shot them with sleeping darts too. Had they been just any old wolves, I would have left them there, but both are sons of Alphas so I thought it wise to have them guarded until they woke up, and then they can return to their homes. I have sent a message to the King of Alphas condemning the Skylander and the Skully packs' action by the Wolf Temple and to warn him against letting it happening again."

"You messaged their King? Threatening him? How did he respond?"

"He hasn't yet."

He probably hasn't stopped laughing.

He doesn't care what the Fae people think and he is most definitely not threatened by a message from the Courtess.

It was as if the world had gone crazy from the moment Father had died.

"I'll send for the maid to bring you new clothes. Let me know when you are ready and we shall commence our travels."

She turned for the door and as she walked out, the guards followed her. I peered out into the corridor and discovered that no guards had been stationed outside my door this time. Maybe there was a guard change or they were going to come back with the maid. I didn't care what the reason was, this was my chance to get out of the room unseen to search for the grimoire.

I closed the door behind me and sneaked down the carpet on light feet. I recognised the building's interior now from having visited when I was younger. Her office was in the attic. I sprinted up the spiral staircase and was in pain and out of breath when I reached the top. I had to pause as I panted with my hands on my knees. When I calmed down, I entered her study quietly, finding myself in a giant room like an ant in a tall jar. There were four sand-coloured pillars placed square in the middle of the room, holding up arches that bridged the vaulted ceiling. Tall wooden bookcases lined the walls and on the top shelf sat statues depicting dignitaries of many centuries past.

A short distance before the window was a massive desk holding a book stand. I sneaked closer to inspect the book that was spread out wide on it and which the Courtess must have been in the process of reading currently. The script on the gold lined pages was ancient with lots of swirls, making the letters hard to read. I carefully flipped over the book to see the cover.

The Fae Grimoire.

I stood stunned.

What bloody luck.

Or maybe it was always in this place. I flicked through the pages faster now, trying to find anything about the blood spell. Blood red text caught my eye. At the top of the page at almost the end of the book I read the heading Blood Curse.

My heart pounded faster. I had found it. All I had to do was copy the information and I didn't even have to steal the grimoire. There were pens and note blocks just in front of me. It was fate!

Suddenly, I heard the pounding footsteps of soldiers marching up the stairs.

Demon Dogs.

I was never going to have the time to write all of this down.

So much for fate having waited for me to be here.

In the panic, I decided to rip out the page. I lifted up my nightgown and shoved the folded piece of paper down my undergarments just in time before the door was slammed open.

"Fae Queen, what are you doing up here?"

Shit, shit, shit! What was I going to do now! I had no good answer to that.

CHAPTER 26

I turned some pages over from the spread with the torn page so it wouldn't be immediately detected. My speech stuck in my mouth, I didn't know what to answer.

Was there any logical reason as to why I was up here? Other than stealing secrets. I was forced to use woman's best weapon.

"I remember being up here once with my father. We were standing right here..." I started sniffling. "And now he's gone." I opened up to let the tears flow and sobbed a bit louder even than I would have if I had had a spear sticking through my gut.

I hadn't realised how real my tears were until then. They weren't entirely fictitious and came easily, rolling down my cheek.

The guards appeared uncomfortable with my display and were twisting and turning, not knowing how to deal with the situation.

"The chambermaid is waiting in your room, my Queen," the first guard muttered under his breath.

Waiting?

If she had planned to help me dress, she would notice the page stuffed into my undergarments. I needed privacy.

I eased off my sobbing and dried my tears. What in the world could I say to get rid of my chambermaid without getting her fired? Simply ordering her away would seem peculiar.

I walked slowly towards the guards, trying to think of something, but drew a blank. They parted to let me pass and take the lead, marching in heavy thumps behind me. It sounded like repeated knocks on the Demon Dog's door. The one cursed wolf who had been banished to the pits of the underworld by the Holy Fae Mother, and who fed on all evil souls – wolf or Fae alike.

I was looking down, feeling as low as the floor when I entered my bedchamber. The guard shut the door behind me. My gaze wandered towards the desk to find Kerri standing there.

My Merry Kerri. My big nosed, flat chested, teal robe wearing Kerri, with a half-bun sticking up from the rest of her loosely swaying long hair.

I wanted to scream, laugh and cry all at the same time. It was my own chambermaid. She wore her signature look that said not to fuss when she worked her magic to display my vanity. Many times, she had playfully told me she had a reputation to uphold.

I ran into her arms. "I'm so glad that you are okay, and that you are here."

"Only the best will do for the queen!" She took a

step back as she snapped her finger and placed the other hand on her hip. "You'll have to stop that sobbing though; you're ruining the base for my work. Just look at your skin…and your hair." She held up a bunch of my hair and ran her fingers down it. "You need oils, and lots of it. What have you been doing? Surviving in the wild, fighting wolves?"

I dried my happy tears. "Yeah, something like that."

"Holy Fae Mother, you look awful. Don't worry, my Queen, it's nothing I can't fix. You'll be brand new in no time…well maybe in about a week, anyway."

The way the word Queen rolled off her tongue felt unnatural. All my life, she had always called me Princess.

She lifted up a red dress that had been lying over the backrest of the chair and displayed it in front of me.

"This is the absolute latest design by Marieaire Dolonique."

I felt the embroidered fabric. "It's beautiful."

The delicate flowery pattern was almost hidden unless you looked closely; from further away it just looked like the dress glimmered with a ruby thread. It had partings over the legs, made for riding and a black studded corset to support my waist. It stated that I was a damsel but not in distress – I could handle myself. There was a new pair of burgundy leather gloves and some jewellery. Oh, how I had missed wearing jewellery; I felt naked without it. Even the leg holster for my knives was fashioned with jewelled chains. I loved the look Kerri had picked out for me.

She stared at me again, seeming to hesitate

before dressing me.

"I'm kind of loving that nightgown though. Can we nick it?"

"Steal from the Courtess?"

Kerri waved her hand in front of her face. "No, no, no, probably not a good idea. Okay, flail out your bosom." With one large sweep, she slid my nightgown right off.

I laughed so hard, I had forgotten about the page until she looked at me oddly.

"Why do you have a piece of paper in your undergarments?"

"I need it for a trade to save my life. Please, don't tell anyone."

Kerri gasped placing her hand over her mouth. "You stole it from the Courtess!"

"Shush!"

"That's it! I'm keeping the nightgown."

She squeezed the gown into a ball and hid it under other garments at the bottom of the travel chest that she had brought with her.

I giggled, relaxing my nerves somewhat, as I didn't know what to expect anymore. Her reaction could have gone either way.

Kerri finished dressing me, tightening my corset, clasping on the jewels and applying makeup. Every now and again she inhaled through closed teeth, obviously at the sight of my injuries, but she never commented or asked any more questions about what I had been through. When she was completely done and I looked at myself in the mirror, I actually felt like my royal self again; an impossible thought only days ago.

We were escorted by the Beetle Guards to the

courtyard, where a black carriage with four black horses was waiting for us. I pushed the red velvet curtain aside as I stepped in, closely followed by Kerri.

The last of the packing was bundled up at the back and it was chunky by the sounds of their struggles. The wheels started screeching not long after, as they rocked us over the cobblestones. I was so happy that there was only me and Kerri in the cabin. I could finally breathe again.

"So, how are things at the castle?"

I had avoided the question for far too long already.

"Not much has changed, other than everything being run with fear and an iron fist. The four court members stepped in immediately. You know Jarminne, if she could have crowned herself queen she would have."

"She would make a great queen."

"Hey! You're queen. She would be awful, having everyone scrub the floor wherever she walked and punishing you if seen smiling. The birds wouldn't sing, the sun wouldn't shine and the river would run as dry as she is. It would become too cold as I walked around breaking all her rules in the nude, like I totally would, so that whenever she wanted she could kiss my ass!"

"Thank you, Kerri," I giggled. "You always know how to make me feel better. What about the other three court members?"

"They are just following Jarminne around like puppies. I think Brimmer tried to hint they should wed to make their claim stronger, but obviously, Jarminne wants world domination all to herself."

I couldn't help laughing out loud.

"And Helsie and Alcar?"

"Helsie has been strutting around Hammon."

"The Master of Coins?"

"Yes, not sure if her affection is genuine or just to line her pockets since she can't seem to take any power off Jarminne. Alcar has not said much. I'm not really sure what side he is on. The Dungeon Master is as creepy as always and you already know what happened to the Commander of the Guard."

"And Clarence," I sighed.

"She disappeared; everyone was wondering where she had gone. Was she with you?"

"She is in Master Crowland's employ; I met her there. She shoved a tray into my chest and laughed as I was crawling for crumbs on the floor."

"Master Crowland? What were you doing there?"

"Long story, that started with a blade to my throat and ended with a fight against the Skyland Alpha."

"Master Crowland, Alpha Moon, Clarence and now you have to go home and deal with the court members; you've not had a great time."

"And my father died."

"Oh, I'm so sorry, my Queen, that as well. I didn't mean to bring that up."

"Don't worry about it. Have you heard anything from Andreas?"

"No. Your bodyguard and the Commander of Guards have been retrieved from the battlefield, but they never found Andreas's body."

There was a span of silence. I looked out of the window and saw Fairola Castle up ahead with its glorious golden arch, the pink keep and the blue rooftops. It would be the first time in my life that I would be going into the castle without my father, he had always been at my side. I swallowed a lump of grief. At least I was home. It was a beautiful day with blue skies and the water around the castle glimmered in the sunshine.

Daytime. Blake was a wolf now.

"Did you know that Blake had a crush on me when we were young?"

Kerri smiled. "Yes, of course; It was obvious, and there was that time when I helped dress him when we were about fourteen. He was practicing how to greet you in front of the mirror, trying out his manners. He looked so silly, I thought that tiny boy with far too soft hair and a perpetually serious gaze would never stand a chance with you but look at him now, quite the catch."

"If you were a wolf."

"Yes, of course, if you were a wolf that is."

It didn't look as if she meant it.

"Why have you not mentioned it to me before?"

"I didn't think it was relevant. As you said, he is a wolf, and you are not."

I sighed. Why did I feel this heavy lump in my stomach? It was almost as if I wanted a part of me to be wolf but that was stupid. I was the Fae Queen.

When the wheels of the waggon crossed the path from the earthy track onto the cobblestones, the noise drowned out my thoughts and the ride became far more bumpy.

The carriage came to a halt in the inner courtyard where an audience had gathered. Everyone was expectantly waiting to see me come out of the box, as if I was back from the dead. The four court members stood at the front of the crowd with faces like stone and I bet to myself that none of them were happy about me being back. The train of my red dress poured out as I descended onto the iron mid-air step and a soft breeze pushed the light fabric to the side. It was weird. I was at home, but I still felt like a stranger; so much had changed in only a few days.

Jarminne approached cautiously, her heavy cloak slithering at her feet; the dark red look giving me the chills. She bore a smile that didn't touch her eyes, making it clear that she was disappointed I was alive. They had all dressed formally with a golden crest around their heads and swords hanging at their waists, marking out only a vague line between showing superiority or respect towards me.

Jarminne performed a deep curtsy. "We were overjoyed to hear of your safety, my Queen."

Heck, you were!

"Thank you, Jarminne. I heard you've done great work in my absence."

"You must be exhausted from your travels. Kerri, see to it that the Queen gets everything she needs at once."

Is she bossing me around already? No way!

"We have urgent matters to discuss. I want the court to convene this afternoon."

Jarminne grabbed a hard hold of my arm and pulled me in for a tight hug with her mouth close to my ear.

"If this has anything to do with wolves, I'll make sure you're forced to abdicate the throne and spend the rest of your life scrubbing floors."

I felt like an ice-queen after she had finished hissing at me, frozen and pale. To ask for permission to help the Alpha lift the curse wasn't going to be a popular topic, I'd realised that, but I had not expected this level of threat.

CHAPTER 27

"And even that, I would be better at than you,"
I hissed back at her.

My heart was burning with rage at their disloyalty
but I had to ensure that I kept my head cool, as I
knew I was already in so much shit for biting back at
her. I doubted I had put her in her place in a way that
wasn't going to result in me cleaning on all fours and
I had a good mind to bawl out to the guards to take
the court members away and chop all their heads off.

I raised my hand into the air, waving a royal
greeting at all the guards lining the battlements, at all
the nobles spectating from their balconies and to all
the other servants who had gathered around whilst I
was putting on a great big smile. Everyone started
cheering and the spearmen tapped their shafts on the
ground, which triggered the swordsmen to bang their
blades on their shields. If Jarminne had planned to

voice any further hostile remarks, she couldn't now with the surrounding noise overpowering all conversation. I felt empowered by the grand reception. Up until now, I had felt like an outlaw runaway peasant, but now, I stood straight up posing like the queen I was.

With royal steps, I advanced into the castle and immediately inhaled the nostalgic smell of pine. The guards behind me marched in unison as we all carried on up the staircase. I didn't even have to open the door to my own chamber as one of the guards leapt in to do it for me, accompanied by a smart salute.

"Dismissed!" I called to everyone crowding my room. "Kerri, I need a bath."

She nodded with a big smile and bowed herself out of the room behind the others, closing the door behind her.

I looked around my room. It almost felt too big and too extravagant for any one individual. Frescos adorned the walls and ceiling, executed by the most talented artists in the land and a huge chandelier hung in the middle of the room, lighting up the two massive sculptures of naked fae playing instruments that stretched from above the mantelpiece to the ceiling. I traversed the enormous rugs crisscrossing over the red carpet, but didn't step on the wolf skin that lay paws spread on the floor in front of the fireplace. I had stomped on it with dirty feet hundreds of times, wrestled with it and had countless tea parties with my dolls causing milky-brownish stains, but never had I ever taken so much note of it as I did now. It felt like someone had skinned my lover alive and placed him in my room so that I would always remember who our enemies were. I thought of Blake

and the promise I had made to him and let out a sigh.
To collaborate with a wolf required court approval
and how could I convince the court members to let
me help him? How could I bring it up without losing
my own head or having to scrub floors for the rest of
my life?

I had aimed for my bed but diverted to sit down
on the window seat instead. Before me I had the view
of the castle gardens and I could also see a vast forest
spreading into the horizon beyond our walls. A sight I
had seen at least once every day growing up. Yet, this
whole place felt like just another building and no
longer my home without my father around. Even the
wolves' den had felt more of a home than this did.
The thought of that felt like a betrayal to my people.

I was startled as Kerri swung open the door and
ordered four strong red coats to push in the bathtub
and leave it in the centre of the room. When the red
coats left, in came a dozen of maids who carried
buckets of steaming water to pour into the bathtub.
The lavender scent reached my nose, I craved to
envelop myself in the soft oils and bury my face into
the bubbles. When there was only Kerri and I in the
quietness of my chamber, she helped me to undress
and held my hand as I walked up the steps that Kerri
had placed next to the tub and slowly submerged
myself into the hot water. Kerri soaped up the sponge
and moved it gently along my scabs and bruises. I
closed my eyes so as not to look at her own eyes,
which were watering from grief.

The span of silence remained until she cleared
her throat.

"They have finally been able to collect your
father's remains. There will be a funeral in the North

Temple the day after tomorrow. They are still…puzzling back the pieces of him."

I didn't look up at her. Images of him being squashed by that boulder played on repeat in my mind.

"Sorry, I said that wrong, didn't I? I hate being the bearer of bad news. I'm not good at it. Don't worry, I'll be right by your side…unless you mention the wolf thing at the courts this afternoon and start a war. Then I will be by your side when we are on the run instead."

"Kerri!" I flung up sitting in the bathtub. "That's not your place to say. When have you ever involved yourself in politics?"

"I know. I know. But this time it's different. You've just come back home, the trust and support you have is fragile and I'm your friend. Just…just lie low for a while."

"That's your advice on how I should rule my kingdom? To lie low?"

The temperature of my blood was already hot in this tub, but boy could it get hotter.

"You have no obligations to the wolves. They are wolves!"

I flung my finger towards the door. "Get out!" I had no clue as to why I felt as heated as I did.

Kerri shrunk back, wide-eyed and gasped. "I just want to…"

"Get out!" I put more strength into my voice. "Get out, get out, get out!"

She put the sponge down on the step and shuffled her feet along the floor. In the doorway she turned filling her lungs. "I know you are thinking of Blake but…"

"Out!" I took the dripping wet sponge and heaved it across the room.

Kerri quickly closed the door to shield herself before it whacked her in the face. The sponge left a dark wet mark on the wood before it thumped to the carpet.

I didn't want to hear any of it. I didn't want anyone to speak ill of the wolves or connect me in any way to Blake. I still felt rough having lost my father; my roots. I had to first figure out who I was and who I wanted to become.

Everything has changed! Everything has changed! Everything has changed!

I had now also had an argument with the only friend I had. I fell back in the bath, almost whacking my head against the rim. Had Kerri mentioned the North Temple?

Great!

At least no one knew that I was the one who had stolen the scroll, which was currently residing in Blake's pocket – if he was still alive. The Courtess had not made that point clear.

Something twisted in my stomach.

What if he was dead?

Well, then all my problems were solved, right?

My stomach still didn't want to settle. Maybe I was just nervous about the court hearing.

Suddenly, there was a knock on the door and it opened ajar. My hopes increased that Kerri had already forgiven me, but it was the seamstress who poked her head in before rolling in a mannequin dressed in my court furs.

"Leave them by the dresser." I didn't even look at her twice.

My heart was so heavy, as I glanced at the court furs and the long black wig – official clothing that my mother had once worn as queen, and her mother before her. It was now my turn to live up to its expectations. My simple princess dress had been exchanged for a long red-coloured fur dress with a wide cotton hem, and there was all the gold and glory to go with it; a hefty tiara, belt, necklace and the royal scroll which I had to hold and swear to tell the truth over, and to act in the best interests of my people – the Fae people.

After a long deep breath, I got out of the bath and wrapped a big white towel around myself.

A young girl who I had never seen before entered the room holding a large tray, which she placed on my table. She didn't even look at me or say anything before she scurried out again, looking frightened. I went over to the table and saw the usual food that I had requested be brought to my room; wine, cheese, bread and grapes. I munched on some grapes whilst I thought about my imminent retaliation in the court house.

I poured myself some wine. "Okay, let's do it," I muttered before taking a sip.

It was time to conquer the dress. I walked up to the mannequin as if I were about to shake its hand and glowered at all the layers I had to put on in the right order. This wasn't going to be easy without Kerri and I pushed out a breath between pouting lips.

I hadn't managed to fully push my hair into my wig, nor had I attached my long cape by the time the chamberlain stepped into the room and cleared his throat.

"The court is ready to receive you now, my

Queen."

The middle-aged man wore his long black court robe and a tight headgear on top of his shaved skull. His enormous livery hung around his neck, held together by flat square chains that blacksmith Fromier's grandfather had crafted.

"Thank you, Mirier. I'm ready." I wasn't.

If you weren't on unfriendly terms with the Courtess before, you would be if you turned up late to a court hearing. No one was late to court. Ever! I had to hurry; I needed to keep the Courtess on my side. It was the only chance I had, considering the topic I was about to raise in front of all the dignitaries in the kingdom.

CHAPTER 28

The court bells chimed ominously as I walked down the aisle towards the seat of power; the First Throne. The First Throne was a great big spectacle on the right-hand side of the Courtess's counter, featuring large porcelain wings emerging out of a red upholstered seat.

Bells announced my arrival as had the trumpet that had sounded the royal fanfare as I walked into the hall. The mood was subdued; no one smiled nor leaned in to spread gossip into one another's ears as everyone stood up in my presence.

All eyes were on me. My nerves were shaking like a rattlesnake. I could almost imagine the sweat pooling down my forehead after having hurried to be on time. I walked past the guards holding tall swords and the healers who were prepared with long yellow cords should any of the discussions in the court hall become heated.

I made sure that I lifted my feet and all the layers of my dress as I ascended the golden step to the First Throne. I graciously turned around and elegantly lowered myself onto the seat, keeping a straight back. I glanced at all the people who were gathered and my breath caught in my throat.

Gosh, this is intimidating!

I noticed clearly how my heart started to beat harder and faster; heat spreading to my head and sweat to my palms.

The Courtess entered from the back room in her long red cloak with two Beetle Guards behind her, and took her seat at the bench, which everyone else took as a sign to sit down, even the four court council members sat down at the bar opposite me. Jarminne was wearing her black court tailcoat as the head councillor and to her left sat Brimmer, Helsie and Alcar in their red jackets. They were all wearing black wigs, which were tied in a neat bow that allowed a tail to run down their backs.

The Courtess's face was devoid of emotion, her piercing, light-green eyes' stare stabbing each court member in turn, nailing them to their seats. The tension was palpable. It wasn't often that a queen had summoned the court; it was usually done by the common Fae who wanted to resolve disputes between neighbours or traders. The court members were going to see this as an opportunity to push me out onto the streets and into the gutter.

The Courtess banged her gavel on the table. "The court hearing has officially commenced. Only one matter has been put to the court by our Fae Queen of Fairola Kingdom. Please, my Queen, go ahead and present your matter."

I twisted in my seat; Demon Dogs, every grain of my body wanted to end this hearing as quickly as possible. I took a calming breath.

"During my captivity with the wolves, I entered into a duel with the terms that if I lost I would assist the Alpha in reversing a blood curse my father placed on him. I gave him my word and I'm asking for the consent of the court to keep my promise."

Oh, and not just that, I also don't want to start a war!

An audible gasp echoed through the audience. Whispers hissed from sharp tongues. I hadn't expected them to like my enquiry and now, I needed to win them over, but how? Their expressions were tense with anger. It was clear that they all thought it was an outrage to have even suggested it.

"Order in my courtroom!" the Courtess shouted, banging with her gavel before turning to the four council members. "What is the court member's counsel on the matter?"

Jarminne stood up first. "Our ancient laws have always forbidden any collaboration with the wolves, which our late king also seemed to have forgotten. I say the Fae Queen must reinstate the traditions in our culture that have been lost, and decline the Alpha's request."

The Courtess looked my way as soon as Jarminne had sat down. "How does the Queen respond to the first counsel?"

Normally, the summoner would stand, but as I was on the First Throne I stayed seated and filled my lungs to ensure my voice amplified enough.

"I will put it to you, and to all the Fae in this room that Jarminne's statement is from archaic times.

Father, our late king, was not wrong in hosting diplomatic gatherings, inviting the wolves to try and bring peace or truce agreements between our kingdoms. I fear that all his work will be cast to the wind if we damage the trust he built."

I saw some Fae nodding in the audience. At least a bunch of them seemed to have bought my argument.

The Courtess invited the next court member to speak and Brimmer stood up, his black hair and square nose not adding anything of comfort to his appearance.

"Perhaps with time, our Queen will gain the experience her father had and be able to collaborate with the wolves, but I believe it to be too soon into her short reign at the moment. I wouldn't want her to be taken advantage of. I say you must decline."

He sat down and the Courtess looked at me.

"How does the Queen respond to the second counsel?"

I had no response. What he was stating was probably true even though I didn't want it to be right and it had made me appear as weak as I felt just then. My mind was devoid of witty answers, so I recited the protocol.

"I graciously thank the court member for his wise counsel."

Without judgement or comment, the Courtess turned to Helsie. "What is the third court member's counsel on the matter?"

"For obvious reasons, I say you must decline."

She had been off and back into her seat before I had the chance to blink. Helsie's butt-licking tongue was so far up Jarminne's bottom, I had not expected any other insight. Her blunt answer offered no opportunity to retaliate either.

"How does the Queen respond to the third counsel?"

"I graciously thank the court member for her wise counsel."

Lastly, it was Alcar's turn to give his counsel. His words were going to sting the most as he was unbiased and known for his harsh but fair judgement. After the Courtess had passed the word over to him, he rose up from his seat so slowly it was tantamount to torture. It was almost as if he hadn't made up his mind yet. He was still quiet when fully standing and looked me straight in the eye.

What was going through his mind?

If at least he was on my side, I could get away with ignoring the others' counsel. All I needed was one vote in my favour.

Please, please, please!

As he didn't speak, the Courtess looked up from her note taking. "Does the fourth court member wish to withhold his counsel?"

He broke the eye contact with me to respond to the Courtess. "No, my Lady Courtess, I will give my counsel, as is my duty," he answered stoically and paused for a long moment once more. "I'm not taking my counsel lightly. This is a predicament seeming without a good outcome and it is my belief that if our queen comes into the claws of the wolves once more, she will be tortured the same as the last time. They can't be trusted. If breaking her word means they will wager war on us, so be it. We can't be bullied into peace, for that peace is not freedom. We should instead strengthen our protection against them until they bend the knee to you, my Queen."

It was like a punch in the gut. Alcar had twisted it so that the counsel seemed to be for my benefit at the same time as he had created an increased fear and hatred towards the wolves. How could I argue with that? I glanced at the dignitaries who sat with their pompous arses on the beautifully carved pews, staring intently at Alcar. I also saw Merry Kerri's head pop out into the aisle from one of the pews at the back to wave at me. That gave me the strength I needed.

As the Courtess raised her gavel to announce an unanimous counsel, I stood up. She lowered her gavel without making that final sealing bang.

"Thank you for your counsel, however the crown will attest that the trust of the Queen's word shall not be questioned. I want everyone to know that when I give my word, my word will be done."

An unanimous gasp rode on a wave over all the pews once more. I wanted to cringe but kept my expression rigid so as not to lose face. It was obviously a strange thing that I was both in the position of summoner of the hearing and the overruling crown. It made it into a case I couldn't lose, having overexerted my royal powers.

Jarminne flew up from her seat, angry as a bull. I could almost see the puffs of frustration streaming out from her flaring nostrils.

"Preposterous, we do not help wolves! Maybe she has promised the Fae crown to the Alpha too. Who knows? She is not fit to reign. Guards seize her! Place her under guardianship until we know for certain that she can be a good queen!"

The guards started stirring but looked unsure as to how to proceed. Of course, this had been

Jarminne's strategy all along. She planned to rule the court and the kingdom as long as I was under guardianship, and I doubted I would ever be released from it alive.

In the havoc of chattering Fae, guards who nervously twisted and clattered their armours together and Jarminne who screamed at the top of her lungs, the Courtess smashed the gavel on her desk to grant Jarminne's claim.

Why had she done that to me? I thought she was serving me well. It truly showed she held the most power in the Fae kingdom because at her order the guards were headed my way.

CHAPTER 29

The guards grabbed hold of my arms and shoved me down the aisle towards the winged doors to exit the court. I struggled all the way, screaming and fighting to get free. One of the younger guards jammed his elbows into my diaphragm in an effort to shut me up.

It worked.

I lost air and folded double, but was held upright by the brutish men. Then, through vision blurred by mountains of fur, I saw dozens of wolves burst through the doors, growling menacingly. At the front of the formation was Blake with eyes that could kill as he focused in on the guards who were manhandling me.

The dignitaries scrabbled towards the walls on the pews as the wolves proceeded further into the court. The Fae were looking at them as if they were monsters from the underworld sent by the Demon Dog and who had come to curse them all. The red caped guards around me drew their swords, pointing them at the approaching wolves. Blake's growl came from so deep inside him, even I stepped back with the guards.

Like a well-trained army, every wolf knew what to do. They attacked as a pack with Blake at the forefront, flying forwards with his jaw open and clutching it around the wrist that held mine captive. The guard hollered in pain and let go of me. Blake gave a sharp bark at me as if to prompt me to follow him, so I did. Whilst the rest of his pack held the Fae at bay we sprinted outside. Kerri was there, waiting for me, on top of a black stallion with an outstretched hand. I ran to her, took her hand and with her help, I hauled myself up behind her as she kicked the horse, urging it on and out of the courtyard. We galloped away from the castle, deeper and deeper into the forest.

"What is going on, Kerri?"

"We are saving your life, my Queen." She made a quick turnaround to flash me a big smile.

"We?"

"Blake, the pack and I."

I tightened my grip around her waist. "Thank you."

Her bravery had cost her dearly. She had made a choice which would change her reputation from that of an outstanding chambermaid to a fugitive of the law. I needed to make it up to her and somehow reinstate both of our reputations. It was the four court members who stood in my way as I doubted that the entire kingdom was against me trying to achieve peace with the wolves.

We galloped through the jungle, with dozens of wolves running alongside us on both flanks.

"What's the plan now?"

"Blake is taking us back to Skyland City."

"We can't go there, Alpha Moon will kill me."

"Blake promised me you were going to be safe, and I trust him."

We are trusting wolves with our lives now? My situation must be really bad.

We reached the river that divided our territories and the wolves stopped to drink. It took a moment before the two of us dared to slide down off the horse's back, and even after that we moved with gentle steps past the pack. I dipped my hand into the ice-cool river and patted my palm along my warm neck, kept hot by all my court furs. I tore my dark wig off and chucked it to one side. I never wanted to wear it again. If I was ever going to be able to claim back my throne, things would have to change; no more hiding behind wigs or fur. There would be no more open court hearings for counselling and I would choose members who I trusted to advise me. Jarminne would be finished!

Kerri came up beside me. "You seem deep in thought, my Queen."

"Nothing." I shook my head. "Thank you for being a true friend."

She scoffed. "Don't be such a sob pouch. This is nothing. You'll soon get back into the castle, kick the court members' arses and rule Fairola Kingdom. You'll see. And Blake will help you. Right Blake!"

Blake was resting a short distance away but lifted his head and barked to answer Kerri. It was weird, even in wolf form they were so civilised yet appeared so wild. It was as if all the discomfort I used to feel being around them had gone and I didn't care that none of the wolves seemed to have any thought about shifting into human form to talk to us and let us know what was going on.

Suddenly, Blake got up and barked at the others, as if he had timed how long they were allowed to rest. At a slower pace this time, we trotted onward and by the time evening was approaching we had made it all the way to the edge of the Skyland City. Blake gave another bark, which sent all the wolves scurrying off, leaving only Blake to watch us. He lowered himself to the ground, hiding into the long grass. At first, I wondered what he was waiting for, but as he kept looking up into the sky, I realised he must be delaying our advance until the curse turned him human again.

Kerri and I dared to sit down next to him, watching the city lights sparkling brighter as the sky turned darker. In the shimmer of the moon, Blake started turning. The hairs on his body submerged, giving way to tanned skin, then paws fledged out into feet, and his ears and nose changed into his recognisable human face. He headed for the bags hung over the black stallion's rear to dig out a black pair of linen trousers and put them on before he turned to me.

"Please, remove your fur cloak, it makes me uncomfortable that you're wearing one of my brothers."

The thought dawned on me, making me dizzy. Of course, I was. I had never thought about it in that way before and now it repulsed me.

I hurriedly unbuckled the pin jewel and shrugged

the cloak off my shoulders. Nervously, I fiddled with my fingers and looked up at him.

"I'm so sorry, I'll never wear fur again."

"Good. Let's go then." Blake strode over the high grass and towards the wolves' city.

I jogged after him. "May I remind you of what happened the last time I visited your home."

I wanted to point out all my scars and bruises that I hadn't had time to heal with a cord yet, but there was no point as he wasn't looking back at me.

"You may, but I do remember and if you want to spare your preaching, I have a feeling you'll be reminding me again soon enough."

With bare feet and without seeming bothered by the dry prickly grass, he continued walking with an intense focus towards the castle. I wanted to pull my hair out, not sure whether it was wise to follow him or whether I should run the other way.

A royal fanfare tuned out from the city and Blake quickened his steps. "Oh, I should be there by now. Hurry up girls, the king doesn't like to be kept waiting."

"The king?" I almost choked on my words.

"Yes, the King of Alphas."

"What is he doing here?"

"I invited him."

I fell into step next to him. "Care to explain why? I've heard he isn't good to have around, his rule being superior to all the other Alphas."

"I told you that your preaching would re-surface." He tilted his head to look at me with a cheeky grin.

What was he up to? I wasn't going to get a pardon to stay with the wolves, if that's what he thought. The King of Alphas wouldn't go against Alpha Moon to that extent.

"I think I'd rather chance it in the woods," I stuttered, veering around.

"No, you're not." He grabbed my wrist and dragged me along. "We must do this. I'm not going to let you down."

I looked at Kerri who was close by my side. She just giggled into her hand and nodded.

As I stumbled after Blake, the dry grass rattled under my boots. "Does the King of Alphas know about your blood curse?"

"Yes. I told him everything."

"Oh Holy Fae Mother, I'm dead."

"No, I'm doing this to keep you alive. Negotiating with the Fae court didn't work and I didn't want to take Scratch's advice and start a war, so this is my last resort."

"By doing what? By marrying me off to the King of Wolves?"

Blake halted abruptly, looking at me grimly. He breathed heavily, not liking that comment at all. I stared back at him and with a few moments to think, he calmed down.

"Sometimes, I forget you are a queen. But no, the king has a wife already. She will be here too, so don't suggest anything of the sort to rub her up the wrong way. She is incredibly protective of her way of life."

"And the love of her husband?"

"I'm not so sure she cares about that, but that isn't my business." He kept on walking. "Don't even think about doing something reckless. You know of his reputation, and you deserve someone who cares for you."

My cheeks warmed. I had forgotten that Kerri had confirmed Helena's story that Blake had had a crush on me since we were young.

We approached the city and stepped onto the civilised roads between houses that towered high toward the sky. Down every street we walked and at every turn we took, there were wolf shifters who turned their heads to see where we were heading.

"Excellent!" Blake said as we arrived at the front of the Alphas' residence where the king had only just arrived and was still climbing out of his horse-drawn carriage.

Without hesitation, Blake moved forward to greet the king, clasping hands all the way up to their elbows.

"Thank you for your attendance," Blake said, and gestured for the king to enter their home.

Attendance?

As my gut instinct had warned, this was not just a casual visit. Something serious was going down, and I was in the middle of it.

CHAPTER 30

Blake made no effort to hide my presence, but instead shoved me forward to introduce me.

"This is Athroxane Crawford, Queen of Fairola Kingdom."

The King of Alphas turned his head towards the palace, seeming more interested in getting out of the wind that was sweeping his jaw-length hair across his face.

"Fae," he muttered.

The Wolf Queen however, pinned me to the spot with a hostile glare. There was no need for her to speak her mind; I could tell she hated me just by my title.

Blake led us inside the wolf castle and down a corridor which seemed too narrow and become darker the further we walked. It was quiet; too quiet. Not even a single wolf was howling at the moon tonight. It was as if the whole town had tensed up at the arrival of King of Alphas. They must have known what was going on. Blake opened a door at the end of the hall and a smell of cinnamon seeped out into the corridor. Blake walked in confidently after he had let the King and Queen in. I followed, and as I stepped inside, I saw Alpha Moon looking up from his desk, the ugly scar I had made with the blue cord on his left cheek still raw. His whole face turned into a frown when he saw the company that had entered at Blake's back into a room that looked to be his office.

He stood up reluctantly, seeming to be bothered by the stab wound where I had planted the dinner knife earlier. "My King, Queen."

As soon as he saw me, his face turned to anger. "What is she doing here? Guards! Seize her!"

"Hold it!" the king bawled, making everyone halt.

That was how much control he exuded; no one moved a muscle.

Blake stepped forward. "Father, this is your last chance to co-operate to cease the blood curse. You must promise that no harm will come to Queen Athroxane."

"Last chance, or what?" Alpha Moon's eyes didn't leave Blake. "What? You'll challenge me?"

Blake nodded slowly. "Take some time to think about it, Father. I'll give you until tomorrow night to decide."

What? Blake challenges his father?

I didn't know if that had ever happened before in the history of the wolves. Heirs normally just bided their time until their turn was up. It was extremely disrespectful for a cub to insinuate that his father wasn't a good enough leader.

Alpha Moon grunted, glowering at me as if this was all my fault.

"No, I don't need until tomorrow night to think it over. If you want to challenge me boy, we will do it right now. That's why you've brought our King and Queen, isn't it? I'd hate to see them wait longer than they have to, wasting their precious time on our pack's trivial matters."

He grabbed the knife that lay on his desk and shoved it into his belt, seeming to be ready to go.

"Let's make this a quick affair. I'll see you in the battle ring in a short while, or when you are ready."

The Alpha looked confident, almost tired, as if he was wrapping up his last business for the day.

"As you wish, Father, but the official rules will still apply. I'm not risking you hurting Athroxane behind my back. I can't let you live; we fight until death."

I thought my heart stopped inside my ribcage, and if not, at least it stung like hell. Was Blake really prepared to kill his father? He looked bloody serious about it. Understandably, he wanted to stop the blood curse infecting the blood line for generations to come, but to kill his own father, that was extreme.

I guess Alpha Moon didn't give him another choice.

My heart seemed to stop again at my next thought. What if Blake was the one who died? Alpha Moon was a strong and highly skilled warrior. For some reason I didn't want to imagine a life without Blake, although I wouldn't have to, I would be next to die after that. Not to mention Kerri. I pushed her behind me before addressing the Alpha.

"Please, oh please, Alpha Moon, this fight is not necessary, please let me help you lift the curse."

"Quiet, Fae!" Alpha Moon spat as if I had the same status as a slug. "This does not concern you. I want to see what my son is made of. *He* challenged me! There is nothing that can stop this fight. One of us will die tonight…or maybe two of us."

His grin deepened as he glared at me.

Blake had better know what he was getting himself into, or we would both end up dead.

Blake growled at the remark and seemed to be about to attack his father there and then if it hadn't had been for the king holding out a hand in front of him.

"Save it for the battle ring."

Blake furiously turned on his heel and stormed out of the room. The rest of the entourage followed and it so happened that I lined up with the Queen of Wolves. I tried to put on a smile and make a bond to start some sort of truce.

"It's a pleasure to meet you, Wolf Queen."

She glowered at me and snorted. "Short lived, I'm sure."

She was right, why bother making small talk when I wouldn't live to see the morning.

Kerri though, leaned around my shoulder as she heard the remark. "Why? Are you planning on dying soon?"

Oh no! Kerri is mocking the Wolf Queen!

Blake had warned us not to do that.

"A Fae chambermaid addressing a Wolf Queen? Well, I've never heard of it."

Kerri opened her mouth to retaliate, but I hushed her and pushed her behind me again. Thankfully, we didn't have to walk very far in silence as our ways parted when the guards showed them to the royal guest chamber. I headed for the Sun guestroom as it was the only place I could think of going to.

Blake was pacing outside the door when Kerri and I arrived. He looked so angry, a flicker in his eyes telling me he couldn't think straight.

"What took you so long!" he snapped as he opened the door for us.

"Sorry, we can't keep up with your insanely long strides! Challenging your father? What were you thinking?"

Wearing no more than his black linen trousers he was still panting as if he was covered in winter cloaks in the peak of summer.

"I need air." Before I realised what he was doing, he headed out of the room.

"Kerri, wait for me here." I closed the door behind me to reassure myself that she would be safe and then I jogged after Blake, managing to catch up with him as he kneeled in front of a statue in the garden. I slowed to watch him as I didn't believe he had noticed I was there. As I observed him, it looked like he was praying. I realised that the grass didn't smell as strongly as it had last time I was here. The summer season was rapidly shifting towards winter; a harder time to travel between kingdoms as the carriages commonly got stuck in the snow; Mazzi didn't like to wade through deep snow either. This made me think about my poor mare and where she could be right now. Maybe Scratch had taken care of her, assuming Scratch was alive and well.

I looked up at the stars which were so beautiful without any clouds obstructing them. But a clear night also meant a cold night and I had rid myself of the fur cloak. I wrapped my arms around me and sneaked closer to Blake. He suddenly twitched his head, hearing my advance, but he didn't turn around. I sunk to my knees on the stone base of the statue next to him, staring at it in silence for a while. It depicted a woman protecting a wolf from an attack, maybe from a bigger animal or in battle, who knew. The woman was keeping the wolf safe behind her back with a sword held out in front of her.

Blake was motionless with his hands clasped in front of him and his eyes closed. I didn't want to bother him but our time was precious.

"What have you done, Blake? Why are you challenging your father?"

He let out a deep breath, unclasping his hands and placing them on his knees. He twisted and finally looked at me; his angry eyes were gone and had been replaced by sad ones.

"It's the right thing to do."

I craned my head to see him better. "Right thing to do? For whom?"

"For our children."

"*Our* children?" I startled upright.

He blushed instantly. "Not *our* children. I mean the generations to come. They deserve peace."

I was amused though, unable to refrain from imagining what Blake and my children would look like as half Fae and half wolf shifter; a cute nose, pointed ears, a plush tail and vicious claws.

"And if you ruled, you would make peace between wolves and Fae?"

"Of course. There is no reason for us to fight; we aren't even in the same food chain. We eat meat and you eat grass and such."

"So you do know we are vegetarians…and it's not grass by the way, it's berries, vegetables and nuts."

He smiled and cocked his head. "Same, same."

I rolled my eyes at him and then fixed them on the statue. "So, what is this all about then?"

He also looked up at the stone figure. "It's a history long forgotten. That is the Fae Mother protecting the first Alpha from the Demon Dog."

I inspected the female. It was true she was Fae, I could see the pointed ears sticking out from her hair. "The Fae Mother was beautiful and brave by the looks of it."

"As was the wolf who had jumped to her aid when the Demon Dog attacked her."

"You believe there was a time when they lived in harmony?"

"I believe they were in the woods together, hiding their love, and the Demon Dog didn't like it. But love has no boundaries – it's indestructible."

"But what about the rope she holds around the neck of the wolf?"

"It's not a rope to restrain him, it's a healing cord." He twisted his head to look at me once more. "Things aren't always what they appear to be."

"So what happened? How did it end?"

"Well, because the Demon Dog is not carved into this statue, wolves have assumed just as you did that the Fae have always tried to rule over the wolves and that's why they despise you." Blake pointed at the hand in which the Fae was holding the leash. "It's said that the Fae Mother bound the First Alpha and with her magic she turned him into the Demon Dog, banishing him to the underworld."

"But that is ridiculous, Fae doesn't have that type

of magic. We can only heal or destroy."

"Or make curses."

I rolled my eyes again. "That magic is almost extinct though."

"Not in those times." He nodded at the statue.

"So wolves think the Demon Dog is the Alpha under a curse?"

Blake shrugged his shoulders in response. "There are always two sides to a story, aren't there?"

"I guess that is true. And what are you praying for?"

Blake went quiet, staring at the statue for a long while.

"I pray that when I die, I will be sent to a place where the Alpha and the Fae Mother are allowed to love each other and rule together…and not end up in the underworld ruled by the Demon Dog."

I chuckled. "You won't end up in the underworld, you are far too nice."

He scoffed. "Nice." He looked at me with an incredulous smile. "I'm challenging my father, aren't I? I'm sure that is not what a good son is supposed to do. A good Alpha heir would honour his father and kill you."

With that said, I again noticed the chill of the night upon my shoulders. I wrapped my arms around myself tightly. "So, why don't you? You don't need me alive to lift the curse, you only need my blood."

He stood up abruptly with a serious expression on his face. "You know why. I'm a fool; the First Alpha reincarnated."

"You are not a…"

Someone interrupted me by clearing her throat just behind us. We both looked back and saw Blake's mother standing a short distance away with her three wolf guards around her legs.

Her grim face was fastened on Blake. "Leave Fae, I need to speak to my son."

"Mother! I want you to at least call her Fae Queen when you speak to her if you refuse to speak her entire title."

She came closer with slow steps, laughing mockingly between her teeth. "In the last months, three hundred and twenty-three of my guards have died, I have had to sit through a boring duel, I'm having an inspection visit by the King of Alphas and I will lose either my husband or my son this very night, all because of this one little Fae. 'Parasite' is a more suitable name for her."

"Mother!"

His mother threw a warning arm up in the air to quieten her son. She circled us, her black dress scraping over the grass and her guards shadowing her.

"Would you kill your mother too, to protect this Fae?"

"Mother, it's not like that. She is a queen and protecting her is a diplomatic stance."

"But if she died right now, there will be other Fae Queens to take her place…but there will then not be any reason for you to fight your father tonight; and I would have both my husband and my son alive come morning."

That was true, by killing me right there, right then she had all to gain and nothing to lose; and I may have done the same if someone was threatening my family.

She came closer, forcing me to back up until I felt the stone statue at my back obstructing my way.

The three wolves at her feet were growling menacingly.

CHAPTER 31

Blake placed himself in between us, shielding me from any attack. We looked just like the statue of the Fae Mother and the First Alpha but just the other way around — and Blake didn't have any weapons to protect us with.

"Mother, you will shame our family more than I have if you murder one of the challengers before the duel."

"I'm not planning on killing you son, only the Fae."

"But you'll have to go through me first to do it and you would still be losing a son. I won't look at you ever again if you do this."

She grunted in frustration. "Kramer, take the Fae Queen back to her room," she said and paused as she stared into her son's eyes. "...safely," she added and spread her arms, indicating she was cooperating.

The largest wolf left her side, starting to walk towards the castle. I looked at Blake for reassurance and he nodded for me to follow the wolf. I walked in a wide circle around his mother and the two remaining wolves to catch up with my wolf escort, but made sure I kept my distance. Looking over my shoulder, I saw that the other two wolves looked more at ease with me gone and Blake's mother was hugging him. I understood that she was in an awful situation and didn't blame her for threatening my life. I couldn't fully comprehend why Blake had challenged his father either. Was he that desperate to rid himself of the curse? Why had all of this mess started anyway and why had my father cast that blood curse? Why had my father been fighting the Alpha and why had the Skully pack been at the Wolf Temple in the first place? Nothing made any sense.

When I entered the Sun guestroom Kerri was sitting at the table with the skittish servant.

Of course she was. She could charm anyone's trousers off.

They stopped laughing at the sight of me and the servant swallowed something fast before standing up.

"Fae Queen, do you require anything from the kitchen?"

I would have liked to answer wine, and a lot of it, but I had to stay sharp tonight.

"Are there grapes and bread on the table?" I craned my head but couldn't see.

"Yes, your favourites, Fae Queen."

Awe, he was such a gentleman. I liked him.

"That'll be all."

He scurried out of the room, closing the door soundlessly behind him.

"So?" I wriggled my eyebrows and smiled at

Kerri.

"So what?" She answered as she started clearing the mess on the table, tidying it up for me to come and sit down.

"You and the servant seemed to be hitting it off."

"He is so lovely…and chatty. Guess what I found out?"

"Ah, so that was what you were doing, gathering information, sneaky, and so you!"

"I know, right! Men can be so chatty as long as they are distracted by large curves and bulging boobs."

"And did he divulge anything that will help us survive the night?"

"No, however I did find out that Scratch returned to his pack and I can only guess what that will mean."

"What are you thinking?"

"He will gather an army to march straight for the Fairola Kingdom, obviously. Fighting for your honour but will inadvertently end up slaughtering all of your subjects in the process."

"That's not good news."

"I didn't say it was."

Defeated, I slumped down on a chair and grabbed a fist full of cashew nuts and ate them one by one as I pondered. Kerri sat down next to me. "How are you keeping up with all that Blake stuff?"

I stopped chewing. "We need to flee."

"What?"

"Blake won't win a fight against his father and if we are still here when he loses, they will kill us next. We have to go." I got to my feet. "Hurry," I urged when Kerri didn't seem to react.

She held both her palms up. "No stop, wait a minute. He has done so much for you and you can't just abandon him now. He needs you. He needs to see your face at the arena to know you support him; that it is all worth the risk he is taking. That's how a real queen supports her allies, the allies who love her deeply."

A knot tightened in my chest. She was right. He might do much better if he knew I was there watching.

"What if he doesn't survive? I can't watch that."

"And *when* he survives and becomes the new Alpha of Skyland then you'll need his help to stop Scratch's pack from ripping Fairola apart."

If Blake survived...I didn't even want to think of the alternative.

"He has to make it."

"He will." She stood up and pushed me towards the bed. "And whilst we wait, I'll take care of your face; you have worn those scars long enough."

I lay down and Kerri brought her chair over to sit next to me at my bedside. I tried to breathe calmly but the thought of losing Blake kept upsetting me. Kerri was rubbing her fingertips together to weave a healing cord. The ones she made were so small and the threads so far apart that I barely noticed when she stroked them onto my skin. The transformation she worked though was as if she had applied masses of makeup. When she had finished, I inspected her work in the mirror and it was as if the duel had never happened and all my ailments were gone, except for the throbbing ache in my heart.

Suddenly, the door was flung open and a blue

cape poked his head in. He was an older man, his hair already turning white, but still he was as wide as an ox.

"I've been ordered to escort you to the arena, Fae Queen. Follow me."

That he had titled me as queen comforted me somewhat since that had to mean he was loyal to Blake. Fully aware that no part of me wanted to watch this gruesome event, I had to act more confidently than I felt. I stood up straight and took long assertive strides to follow the wolf guard.

I knew the way to the arena; I had walked it before, yet every step closer to it that I took felt as foreign as a step in the wrong direction. It was way past midnight but the rare event seemed to have roused even the youngest children to stay up.

To make this a small affair! Sure!

The place was packed and the wolf shifters who didn't get a space inside were climbing up the fence around it to get even the slightest glimpse of the battle ring. The crowd that had gathered and were lining the street as we walked past were screaming angry curses at me. Suddenly, a young man broke out from the line and blocked our path.

"I hope they kill you Fae!" he shouted.

The blue cape leading us drew a dagger from his belt. "No one threatens our honoured guest, the Fae Queen of the Fairola Kingdom!"

My jaw almost dropped at the way he had defended me and my name, but the young man didn't move out of his way. Instead, he threw a punch at the guard who ducked out of the way and planted the dagger deep into his shoulder. The young man stumbled back, shock written on his face. He had not expected the wolf guard to harm him in the defence of a Fae, that much was clear.

"No!" I burst out. Kerri and I rushed to his side, helping him to sit on the cobblestones.

In unison, Kerri and I started chanting as we rubbed our fingers hard and fast. "Sinsra livris meris, Sinsra livris meris, Sinsra livris meris."

"Take three deep breaths," I instructed the young man. He focused and inhaled, and as he did I mouthed to Kerri, 'Ready'? She nodded.

Before the young man had exhaled his second breath, I yanked the dagger out of his shoulder and Kerri and I both pressed our cords to seal the wound. I managed not to scream but some agonised noises exited between my clenched teeth as the pain streamed up and down my spine. The young man was brave though and didn't complain at all. He only panted heavily until we had finished. When I was about to remove my hand from his shoulder, he grabbed it and held it still steady over his flesh.

"You saved my life." His voice sounded incredibly disbelieving at what had happened.

I dried some tears that had escaped from the corner of my eye with the pain. "We are not enemies." And then I remembered what Blake had said. "We are not even fighting in the same food chain."

We both chuckled as we looked at one another.

The robust voice of the guard boomed behind me. "Boy, let go of the Fae Queen's hand!"

The young man instantly let go. "Yes, of course," he said, getting off the ground and back into the line where he stood still, looking bewildered.

Did all the wolves really believe like that young man had, that Fae were monsters? Just in the same way that we Fae thought of them.

I hurried after the guard and we entered below the arched walkway leading to the fighting arena. It was the first time I had ever noticed hesitation from Kerri as she grabbed a supporting hold on my arm. I patted her hand to let her know that everything would be alright, even though I knew that was unlikely. The guard didn't seem to veer off towards the back walkway which led to the royal balcony.

"Hey Guard!" I shouted for him. He stopped and turned to look at me. "It's this way, isn't it?"

"That's to the royal balcony."

"I know…I am royal."

"You want to sit at the side of the Alpha's mate?"

"If it's from where I'll have the best view."

One of his eyebrows lifted questioningly. "You do know what she thinks of you?"

"I don't care what she thinks of the King of Wolves himself; I'll show my support for Blake."

The guard looked at me sceptically. "Okay, suit yourself."

The guard led me through a secluded passageway tunnelling underneath the spectator stands. The walls on either side were of dark stone from which spikes protruded as if to prevent any passers-by from straying from the centre. Some of them were coated with dark red on their tips; already blood stained from creatures the Alpha had no longer wanted alive. The creepy sight raised the hairs on my arms and I crossed them for comfort. After having followed the guard for a while, we arrived at the bottom of a short stairway.

The guard didn't put his foot on the step and instead stopped and turned around. "This is where I leave you."

It looked as if the guard was afraid to go any closer to the Alpha's area, and perhaps I would be wise to be terrified too. He walked away in the direction we had come from, leaving Kerri and me to face our darkest fears. I looked up and through a crooked archway to see the navy-blue sky that was speckled with stars. I was fearful that ascending the steps would be like walking towards a dark void that would open up to a world of terror; claws, fangs and angry yellow eyes.

I reached the top, but stopped startled, breathing fast with my heart racing. The balcony was already fully occupied by the King and Queen of Alphas and their guards. The royal couple were seated on the two largest thrones and Blake's mother had been pushed aside to sit on an ordinary chair on the far right-hand side.

The King noticed my arrival and signalled to one of his guards with little enthusiasm. "Get the Fae Queen a chair."

The guard pushed Kerri to stand with her back against the wall as he brought over a chair for me that had been standing against the back wall of the balcony and placed it next to Blake's mother.

My heart pounded so hard it hurt in my chest as I started to walk towards her. Sitting next to her could mean a dagger in my back or even openly into my stomach. It was physically dangerous to sit next to her and if it had been anyone other than the king who had ordered me to sit down, I would have declined.

I supported myself by holding onto the chair as I

reached it, noticing my hands were shaking. Blake's mother didn't greet me nor did she even turn her head to look at me.

Terrified of looking out onto the area where I had almost lost my own life, I took a deep breath with closed eyes to gather courage.

I was startled upright though by a loud fanfare signalling that the gates were closing and the fight was about to start.

The torches were lit with bright yellow fire around the pit as the two fighters marched in. Both of them strode into the arena looking angrier than I had ever seen them before and neither of them stopped to take in the audience chattering. Alpha Moon had taken the lead and Blake was following him closely, his eyes on his father's back. Neither hesitated to step onto the gangplank to cross the moat over to the ring, nor twitched as it was snapped away.

I felt eyes on the back of my neck and twisted my head to see the King of Alphas glowering at me as if this whole thing was my fault. I swallowed and quickly turned my head back towards the duel. The two men were circling the ring barefoot, staring daggers at each other, wearing only leather trousers and an elastic band to keep their hair in a knot at the back of their heads. Bent over, with muscly torsos and raised fists, their concentration was centred on the upcoming fight; only now waiting for the gong to ring so they could start. They would have to jump at each other with all their might to stand a chance as both of them were skilled warriors; but one of them must die.

TO BE CONTINUED…

Printed in Great Britain
by Amazon

15821695R00129